BETTING ON LOVE

ALEXIS ABBOTT

PATHFORGERS PUBLISHING

Get an EXCLUSIVE book, **FREE** just as a thank you for signing up for my newsletter! Plus you'll never miss a new release, cover reveal, or promotion!

http://alexisabbott.com/newsletter

A globe-shaped chandelier hangs from a black ceiling that looks like a more starry night sky than Las Vegas has ever seen. It casts dim light over pristine green carpet with red and pink flower print.

A speckle of blood stains it as I throw a man to the ground after parrying his drunken fist.

"Fuckin'...son of a bitch! I'll sue this fuckin'-"

I reach down and seize the man by the back of his collar and hoist him up, cutting him off mid-sentence. I wrench his arms behind his back and hold him while I stand him on his feet. He tries to struggle, but I have an iron grip on him, even if he does have about 50lbs on me. I move him away from the bar and toward the back rooms so fast and so subtly that the other guests barely have time to notice that I'm dragging him away.

That's my job.

I'm working security for this casino, and I make problems go away.

Two of my enforcers are waiting for me once I get the staggering drunk asshole off the casino floor, and they receive him with the grace I trained them to have, holding him up and steady while his head sways back and forth. After that little burst of aggression and getting tossed to the ground, his head is probably swimming. He'll be lucky if he remembers anything from tonight.

And if he keeps putting up a fight, he'll be unlucky.

"Got trashed off his ass, started harassing some of the female guests, took a swing at my bartender when he tried to cut him off," I explained in my usual curt, no-nonsense tone. "I don't care if he's not on strike three yet. Get him out of here. If he tries to apologize, throw him in a cab and send him to his hotel. If he doesn't, he can sleep it off out back."

"Yes, sir," one of the enforcers says, and they both give me a brief nod before dragging him off into the shadows. I take a breath, then turn around and stride back out onto the casino floor, eyes combing the place for any other fires tonight.

I'm imposing on my own. I usually don't have to raise a fist to be intimidating. People stiffen up when I patrol by, and when my gaze falls on them, they get anxious. I use that to my advantage. When I'm on the floor, as far as I'm concerned, this is my casino.

And I run a tight ship.

It's a Friday, and the sun went down about half an hour ago on this autumn evening that was getting cooler outside by the hour. That means the gamblers are starting to come out in droves, and that means it's time for security to get out in force. The sooner my forces are out keeping an eye on things, the sooner we'll know what kind of night it's going to be. I never let things get out of hand here.

This is a mob casino, and I don't let anyone fuck with us.

Most people are fine. They're just tourists, even the ones who are high rollers. This isn't the kind of place you come in with just a cool $50 to try to blow or invest and make off with a little extra pocket change. People come in ready for the ten-grand minimum, and they're usually the kind of people who consider that chump change.

I watch the steady stream of them coming in through the glass doors. Most of them are older men with younger women hanging on their arms. The men are a mixed bag. Some of them wear suits that could rival my own from some of the best tailors in the world. Others are more relaxed, and I even see a polo or two strolling around. We're not supposed to let that kind of casual outfit through the doors, which tells me those are the kinds of guests who are too important to stop.

These are the kinds of people who see Vegas as just another stopover between their summer home in Monaco and family manor in California. I've even spotted a couple of A-list celebrities making their way through, complete with the big sunglasses and hats that keep them from being recognized too easily. It doesn't happen often, and when it does... I couldn't care less.

I'm here to make sure things go smoothly, and I go home with a fatter paycheck than I could ever need. Fast money, fast women, fast luxury—that's what drew me in, and that's what keeps me working smart and climbing the ladder.

And I'm pretty fucking good at it.

The people who make their way in usually fit a profile. I've gotten good at reading them over the years. Most are couples or groups, heading in for more of a social affair than anything else. Small groups are easy to deal with, because people are usually too interested in each other to get too sloppy drunk. Large groups are a nightmare, easily the most likely to act out. Bachelor parties are a sign that I need to start calling in extra help.

Lone guests are another story.

Some are professional gamblers. They usually slink in and make a beeline for the tables without getting a drink. Those are the ones I need to keep an eye on, because if there's one rule to this place that always holds true, it's that the house always wins. If it looks like that's not going to hold true, I need to *encourage* it to.

But the kinds of people who know how to handle themselves in a casino are careful. The few who fly under my radar are careful not to walk off with too much or draw too much attention. But most telling of all is that they have a certain look in their eyes, something subtle that hints at intelligence, cunning, and simple luck.

Those are the eyes I see when *she* walks in.

Nearly six feet of pure red walks through the doors with the grace of an angel and the emerald eyes of the devil himself. Long red hair spills down her pale, bare shoulders and melds with her crimson, form-fitting dress that hugs her curves and ends just above the cherry-red heels that are giving her those extra few inches, but I can tell she's tall on her own. Her sheer dress gives me a view of those long legs that walk with such purpose, each step knowing exactly where it's headed.

Those diamonds hanging around her neck don't come cheap, either. The starry lighting in the casino makes them glitter the way they were meant to, and she knows it. She has confidence, poise, and taste—even if she's someone's arm decoration, no crusty old fart knows how to dress someone like that.

She sparks my interest.

My first thought is that she's a high-class escort. Women in her profile don't tend to be here alone, they're usually heading to meet someone—some asshole who was either too lazy or too nervous to pick her up from a hotel room. But she doesn't have that searching look on her when she first walks in. She surveys the room as if drinking it all in. I can almost see her mind taking notes.

I'm ex-military. I don't get distracted easily unless I damn well want to get distracted. And even though my cock is stirring between my legs at the sight of this girl, my mind is clear when I decide to follow her at a distance and see where she goes. This is one lead I want to follow through with personally.

Something changes about her as she makes her way through the casino. It's so subtle that I wouldn't have noticed unless I'd spotted her the second she walked in, but it's there. Her hips sway with an almost hypnotic rhythm, and she loses some of the purpose in her step. No, she doesn't lose it—she drops it. She casts a glance around at some of the men in the casino, and I see a bat of her eyelashes that lasts only long enough to make them turn their heads as she walks by.

Everything about her body is enticing people around her to look at it. But I'm no lovesick teenager, and I've seen so many beautiful people walk through this casino that I'm numb to it all by now. There is something different about her, something...measured. She knows what she's doing, I realize.

I crack a smile as I see her head over to the poker tables.

She sidles up along with the rest of the spectators, and they make room for her. Her presence commands attention, even from some of the players. And that's especially impressive, because I know that table to be full of some of the more experienced regulars. I wonder if she did her homework beforehand, if her man is at the table, or if she just has a nose for the real skill in the house. All three options are intriguing.

I follow at a safe distance, pretending to be keeping an eye on the floor around the poker tables while actually keeping my eye on her.

Her body language confirms what I suspected when she walked in. She only tucks a lock of stray hair or adjusts her legs when one of the players is glancing away from the table, and when they do, it's usually at her. I notice her smile at one of them when they make eye contact. Her every move is measured, calculated.

I respect that.

First chance she gets, I watch her buy in, and she takes a seat with the high-rollers, right next to the guy who just won the last hand. She smiles at him, and suddenly, she's a little more animated than before—but not too much so. She can't seem too interested. I feel like I'm getting into this woman's head, and I have to admit, I can see why she looks like she's having fun.

The player she's sitting next to takes to it warmly, but he's not a total sucker. Once the game gets started, things get serious and reserved again, but I see how often the other players glance over at her. How could they not? They're as interested as I was when I first saw her. She encourages them in subtle ways, usually with brief eye contact, just enough to keep them thirsty for more. They're utterly taken by her.

So taken that she wins her first hand.

I see the smiles on the faces of some of the older men. I can practically hear the words "beginner's luck" on the tips of their tongues. They think it's cute that she trounced them the first time around. It even interests them a little. Men like them like girls who can impress them, but not threaten them.

That amusement starts to fade a little when she wins a second time.

By the third hand, the smiles have started to fade from the men's faces, but they're getting challenged. Some of them look like they're ready to get serious, while others look like they're about ready to get up and leave. All the while, the crimson lady hasn't changed. She has a mildly amused, surprised look on her face. I'm pretty sure I saw the actual words "beginner's luck" on those ruby-red lips at one point.

She says what the men are thinking, and that puts them at ease and keeps them going a little while longer. She's clever. Very clever.

But just before she pushes the men too far, I see her cash out, and she gives them all a flirty, ditzy wave before leaving them behind and heading to the bar. The men she left in the dust look at each other with mild surprise, but not anger. She didn't totally wipe them out, but she left the table with far more than any of them could have expected, leaving them with just enough to keep playing instead of complaining to me and trying to chase her down.

They played right into her hand.

I never saw her cheating. The dealer didn't catch on either, if she was. We have subtle signals we can give each other when we see someone cheating at the tables, and as stunning as this girl is, I wouldn't hesitate to do my job if she'd been trying something dirty. But if she was, she was better at keeping it hidden than I was at spotting it.

That is rare.

She didn't fail to pick up some attention on her way out. Some of the guests murmur to each other and nod in her direction, and some of them let their eyes linger on her longer than that. Usually, someone winning that big and drawing that much attention was a big red flag. She managed to skirt around that suspicion, just barely. I have no reason to step in and intervene yet.

But I want to.

I'd be a liar if I tried to pretend I haven't been sizing her up the whole time. Even without the act she's putting on, there's no question that she's a knockout. She's making all the things she was blessed with work overtime for her. And that stride, that confidence, that cunning...it's enticing.

I'm not the kind of man to flatter myself, but I've never had any trouble getting any woman I'm interested. I don't usually do that kind of thing on the job, but I have a little more cause to follow this lead through. There's something just under that sexy surface, and I'm interested in knowing what it is.

She's calculating, but so am I.

Almost as soon as she makes it to the bar Tony is working, I follow her, striding up with every bit of confidence and poise that she does.

Time for me to meet the lady in red.

HADLEY

I certainly did not come here today to meet a man.

In fact, I kind of pride myself on only associating with men who are either paying me outright or who are dumb enough for me to take their money on the downlow. Either way, I had better be getting paid.

As I sit under the rolling purple and gold lights, I know perfectly well how sensual and captivating it looks flickering across my face. Everything about me, both natural and intentional, is perfectly designed to transform me into a trap.

I'm like those sparkly, glittery fishing lures they sell at little shacks by the sea for fishermen. I am a siren, a shapeshifter moving through the tipsy crowds thick with cigar smoke and heady, reckless desire. People don't come to a casino to make bright, brilliant choices. They come here to escape things.

Dark shadows, past mistakes, trouble at home, unhappy marriages, responsibilities stacking up and looming over them like some ravenous beast.

On the outside, any man who walks into a casino can look cool and collected. He can look like he's there for a casual hour of people-watching, to strut around in designer duds and flirt with the pretty blackjack dealer. But trust me, no matter how slowly he seems to be moving, he's actually running. Running away from something. Ready to forget his mistakes by committing brand new ones.

And that is where I come in.

I know what I look like. I am not vain, but I'm pragmatic. I know exactly what my fiery red waves the color of copper wire, creamy white skin, and wide grass-green eyes do to people, and especially men. It's one of the reasons I got this job.

Besides, I'm adaptable.

If a man comes in here looking for trouble, then trouble is what I'll give him. With those guys, all I have to do is show my teeth. They loathe boredom. They long for danger. I can offer all of that in spades. I turn into a vampy seductress, reeling them in and spinning a tight, gauzy web around them until they're totally wrapped up in fantasy.

If a man comes here looking for someone to soften his pain, to give him hope and listen to his list of woes, then that's the part I will play. I can make myself seem gentle, acquiescent, easily molded into whatever delicate, doe-eyed waif he's come hunting for. No matter which mask I wear, I'm always the same serpent underneath.

I'm always sniffing out that payload, it just varies which path I take to find it.

I've always been pretty good at reading people, ever since I was an admittedly precocious child. It is difficult to dissuade me, even harder to fool me. I can see someone's intentions as plainly on his face as his nose or lips. I know how to weasel my way into someone's psyche, dig out the bad stuff and shine a light on it or search out the weaknesses and exploit them.

Even before I went off to college to double major in math and psychology, I was skilled at both of those disciplines.

Math, I learned from a young age, could help me crack just about any problem fate tossed my way. There was always a formula, always an equation to be finessed and balanced. The world was made up of numbers, and I could use my brain as a calculator to navigate through the minefield of being a woman in this day and age.

Psychology, on the other hand, taught me that I could crack just about any problem human beings threw at me.

The two make a happier marriage than even I could have predicted back when I first enrolled in university as a wide-eyed freshman years ago. I outpaced my classmates and infuriated my professors. I began to see numbers everywhere. I could count and add and divide and multiply like a human calculator. It was fun for me, finding the everyday numbers all around me.

I didn't finish school. I was given a much more tantalizing offer: to become a card-counting casino maven, tricking witless men into emptying their pockets onto the table, seemingly summoning piles of red and black chips like an enchantress. Just a snap of my perfectly manicured fingers, and the world spilled out into my lap.

Most of the time, I am not affected in the least by the whims and wants of men. I can see right through them, adding them up to divide and conquer just like I do with a deck of cards under fluorescent lights. The idea of ever meeting a man who could keep up with me, physically or mentally, is a bygone dream.

The more sharply I hone my illicit craft, the harder it becomes to imagine a man who resists the equation. So many of them are so easily reduced to numbers. Even the big, tough, brawny guys in their Range Rovers and limousines and glossy Teslas cannot match my stride. I move too quickly. I think too quickly. I am a chameleon, and if there's one thing I have learned about men, it's that they do not like a woman who's hard to pin down.

But this guy, this devilishly handsome man in a sleek, black designer suit expertly tailored to emphasize every rounded muscle and sharp, lean line of his body, has me admittedly a little stumped. When I look at him, it's a little tricky to find the numbers. He's not easily fitted to an equation. He's more complicated than that, I can tell. I knew that before he even opened his mouth to say something to me.

I have to confess, he makes me just a little bit nervous. That's new. That's unusual.

And yet, I know how to keep my cool. It takes more than just a pretty face and a low, growly voice to unsettle the likes of me. So I give him a tiny but potent gift in return: a smile.

"Can I sit here?" he asks, that voice so deep and rough as a gravel road.

I don't want to seem overly eager, but I can't reveal my nervousness either. It's all about waiting for the right prey to drift into my net without sacrificing my place. So I give him a little shrug of my shoulder, biting my plush bottom lip as I gaze up at him through a veil of thick dark lashes. I nod slowly, never breaking eye contact with this absolute rugged mountain of a man.

"It's a free country, handsome. You can sit wherever you like," I purr, leaning back in such a way that my chest is emphasized and my long waves of hair cascade delicately over my left shoulder. "And with a face like that, I doubt you ever have to ask permission in the first place," I added pointedly.

"Chivalry is next to godliness," he replies coolly, taking the bar stool next to mine.

I raise a perfectly arched eyebrow. "I thought it was cleanliness," I answer.

"Clean is a given," he says. "Chivalry is an art."

"And I bet you think you're very, *very* good at it, don't you?" I tease, a smile playing at the corners of my lips.

"Good enough to have convinced a girl like you to speak to me," he counters deftly.

My heart skips a beat and the sensation is so unusual it almost makes me frown in surprise. But I manage to maintain my trademark aloofness. I won't let the mask slip from my face so easily. This guy may be a slippery fish compared to my usual prey, but if there's one thing I'm never afraid of, it's a challenge.

Most of the time, even when a man works up the courage to approach me, I can feel him quaking in his shiny leather loafers. I have a sixth sense for a man's weakness, the little crack in his armor where the light fights through. It just doesn't usually take me so long to locate it. But I'll be patient. I've already met my dollar quota tonight. The feeding frenzy is over. I have time for a little game of cat and mouse.

Although, judging by the hungry, almost wolfish look in his eyes as he watched me, I'm a little uncertain as to which one of us is playing which role.

"And what makes you think it's hard work to get

a conversation out of me?" I ask innocently, changing my tactic a little bit. Clearly, this man isn't as vulnerable to the femme fatale effect. Maybe he's more swayed by a poor little lost girl. A delicate flower. Sometimes a beast is better tamed by a lullaby than a whip.

He chuckles softly to himself, peering at me out of the corner of his eye as he turns to face the bar counter, preparing to order a drink. "Well, there's nothing especially approachable about a woman with the face of an angel who's wearing red stilettos. I have a feeling most men are a little intimidated by you, right?" he says sagely. And correctly. But I'm not ready to throw out my masquerade just yet. I've got a few cards up my sleeve, still.

"Intimidated? By me? I wouldn't say that," I reply coquettishly, tossing my thick red mane. The guy just smirks at me, his face nigh unreadable. It's a little unnerving, the way he seems to evade my usual psych-out tactics. I keep firing at his heart, but it's like he's wearing a bulletproof vest.

"So this whole siren look is meant to be, what, modest?" he goads me gently.

I smile at him, but I give him a warning with my eyes. I am not to be toyed with. I don't respond, but he doesn't seem to mind or even notice. He gives the bartender a subtle nod to call him over, which is an impressive feat considering how crowded the bar area has become. There are big-spending men dressed to kill, modelesque women in haute couture, all of them clamoring for the bartender's attention, even offering him little bribes of cash in exchange for some service. But my strange new companion hardly has to move a muscle to cut to the front of the queue.

The bartender, a burly guy whose name tag reads ANTONIO in shiny gold lettering, slides down to lean on the counter in front of us. "What'll it be, folks!" he asks.

"Gin and tonic for me," comes the smooth reply, "and a vodka cranberry for my new friend here."

I open my mouth to protest, but realize there's no point. He's right on the money. That is precisely what I would have ordered if given the chance, although usually I prefer to sip tap water while on the job. It's a strategic choice, not a cop-out. Tap water looks like any variety of clear liquor, it keeps me hydrated and looking dewy fresh, and it allows me to stay clear-headed even while my fellow casino-goers get progressively sloppy and loose with their money throughout the night. Now, though, I'm finished with that for the evening, and a vodka cranberry is the perfect sweet ending to my shift.

"You got it, sir," Antonio the bartender says, and immediately gets to work. He expertly pours our drinks and slides them across the bar to us, then asks, "Would you like to start a tab?"

My companion nods. "Yes. I would," he says.

Sipping my drink, I give him a wary look. "That's awfully presumptuous of you to assume our conversation will last long enough for more than one drink," I tell him, hoping my carefully-sharpened words will knock him off his game.

But he seems unperturbed. "Maybe. But you strike me as the kind of woman who would scoff at anything less," he explains. "I'm not cheap."

"Your ensemble tells me that," I quip, looking him up and down.

He smiles and says, "By the way, my name is Dominick."

There it is. I feel a tiny cheer of victory deep in my soul. I always prefer for my men to give themselves up first. "Enchanted to meet you. I'm Naomi," I lie.

My name isn't Naomi, but for tonight, it might as well be. I've learned that a name can be a precious jewel to guard. Not just anyone can have it. They have to earn it.

"Naomi," he repeats, the syllables sounding musical on his tongue. "Not the name I would have guessed, but it's beautiful."

"Thank you," I reply.

"So, Naomi, tell me what it is that brings you to a place like this," Dominick asks, and I can tell he's genuinely interested in the answer. That's strange. Most men don't care.

"What brings anyone to a casino?" I answer with

a playful shrug. "It's the adrenaline rush. The joy of the game."

"I noticed. You're either the luckiest girl in the world or the smartest," he says wisely.

I smile, twirling a lock of hair around my finger. "Can't I be both?" I tease.

He nods slowly. "Yes. In fact, I have a sense that you are many different things, Naomi. I'll bet you're just as comfortable at a casino bar here in Vegas as you would be sitting on a bench at the gardens of Versailles."

Again, I feel my heart skip a beat. How annoying.

"The gardens are lovely," I tell him, toying with the straw in my drink, "but it's the palace that'll blow your mind."

"So, you're into architecture," Dominick notes.

"I'm into all things old and beautiful," I reply. "There's nothing like walking through the vaulted archways of Notre Dame, hearing some centuries-old hymn echoing in the rafters."

"You're well-traveled, then," he points out. "I figured."

I rest my chin on my fist as I look at him, letting my guard slip for a moment. I love talking about the places I've traveled to, especially with someone who doesn't begrudge me the luxury or think I'm some uppity snob for it. I don't travel so that I can boast about it later. I travel because I love to challenge myself, to learn new things, to be a stranger in a crowd for once.

As Dominick and I talk about the places we've been and the sights we've seen, I find myself leaning in a little closer to him, until, two more vodka cranberries later, there are only a few inches left between us. I have never been so magnetically drawn to a man in my life. It's not that he has the upper hand, either. I feel like the two of us are standing on equal ground. I don't have to make myself smaller or taller to fit him. He knows how to mold to my shape, just on instinct.

And I have to admit, I find it completely intriguing.

So when he murmurs, "Should we consider taking our conversation somewhere with a little more privacy?" it isn't apprehension or annoyance I feel. It's excitement.

"I have a room upstairs," I reply in a hushed voice.

Dominick smiles. "Let's go."

I even let him take my hand as he pays the bar tab with a handsome tip and the two of us slip away through the drunken crowds. I wonder if he can hear how hard my heart is beating. I wonder if he can smell the adrenaline pumping through my veins. It takes quite a lot to excite me these days, and generally the only thing that makes my heart thump is the feeling of cold hard cash in my hand. But

Dominick has me longing for something different. Something a little less impersonal. Something intimate.

We make it halfway to the elevator that will take us upstairs when my cell phone starts to vibrate in my handbag. Frowning slightly, I stop in place and take it out, my eyes going wide when I see the name on the screen.

"I apologize," I tell Dominick quickly. "I have to take this."

"No worries," he says, stepping away a few yards to give me some space.

I slide the screen open to answer, pressing the phone to my ear. "Vanessa," I say.

"Hadley," she gasps, her voice sounding frantic and out of breath. "Are you there? Can you hear me? Please god, say you're there."

My heart sinks. This doesn't sound good at all. "I'm here, Vanessa, I'm here. What's wrong? Calm down," I murmur, keeping my voice low.

I hear Vanessa heave a few deep, ragged breaths, and I can positively feel the tears streaming down her pretty face, leaving streaks of black mascara. "I-I'm scared. He hurt me. I don't know what to do. Please—please help me."

I've been standing by the hotel room window, staring out at the alluring white and neon lights of Vegas glowing up at me, pretending to be distracted. I can't help but overhear what the girl is saying, though, partly because I'm in the room, and partly because it's my job to listen.

I didn't believe her name to be Naomi for a second, but I'll go with that for now. Honest guests don't show up at my floor and clean out a table full of professionals for a quick *million*, and they certainly don't take secret calls in their hotel rooms. I've long since abandoned the theory that she's just an escort of some kind.

She's more than that, and that makes her both more dangerous and more intriguing.

Vanessa. I make a mental note of the name, but all I have to go on is what "Naomi" is saying. It sounds like she's friends with this person, or at least close to her in some way. She dropped the name, too, which doesn't seem appropriate for someone as obviously experienced as she is.

I have a few advantages here. First, she doesn't seem to know I'm either security or working for the mob that runs this place. My boss is Jerry Laskin, one of the most dangerous and feared names in Vegas right now. That carries weight, and I can guarantee that if she had a scrap of a hint that I answer to him, she'd be treating me very differently, probably not even engaging with me out of fear I'd catch on to... whatever she's doing. Second, whatever's going on with Vanessa sounds urgent enough that she's dropping her guard, at least a little bit.

Far be it from me to take advantage of a vulnerable woman, but I could get some valuable intel out of this, if I play my cards right.

Or, she could be stringing me along for something even more elaborate. "Naomi" is full of different possibilities, all of them interesting. Regardless, if she doesn't know who I am, I need to keep it that way.

There's a very good reason I'm not dressed like the rest of security and don't like the guests seeing me act like security. She doesn't need to know that reason. Nobody does. Not until my job is done.

"Vanessa, calm—I need you to calm down, take slow, deep breaths like we practiced," she says as I stare out the window. "Where are you?" A pause. "Okay, stay there, I'm on my way. Keep the door locked, don't answer until you see my text and can see me standing outside the door. Okay? Okay, good. See you soon. Breathe."

She clenches her jaw as she ends the call, staring at the phone with a worried look on her face. It's the most she's let her guard down since we first saw each other. A moment later, she looks up at me, and I feel an arrow through my heart.

At first, she looks like she forgot I was there entirely, like I just intruded on a very private, intimate conversation. There's defiance mixed with surprise in those eyes that reflect part of the Vegas skyline through the window. Even so, they're so deep and expressive that I feel my heart thud harder against my chest as our gazes meet. There's something so profound about the way her eyes can lock into mine that for just a second, it makes me doubt whether I'm really in control of this situation.

"Sounds serious," I say mildly.

"I'm sorry, but I have to go," she says, brushing a stray lock of red hair out of her face. "I don't know how much of that you actually heard, but a friend of mine needs me to come see her. I hate to be that kind of person, but..." She pauses, looking me up and down. "Can we pick this up another time?"

"We could," I say, taking a few slow steps toward her. She doesn't flinch, nor so much as move a muscle, even with the dim lights behind me casting an ominous shadow over my figure. I know how intimidating my body can be to most, but "Naomi" is definitely made of something stronger than that. "But if you would like a hand, I know a little muscle can make some problems go away."

"I don't recall saying this was a problem that muscle could solve," she says, cool as ice.

"You didn't," I admit. "But the kinds of problems women like you have in a casino like this tend to be the kind where a little muscle doesn't hurt."

"And what does 'women like me' mean?" she asks.

"The kind who catch my eye," I answer.

Her jaw clenches again, and I can tell she's looking for an excuse to tell me no, so I finally give a soft smile and start to walk toward the door.

"If you're holding out for me to say 'wait', you're going to be disappointed," she says as I walk past her and rest my hand on the door handle.

"How about I just block the door until you make up your mind, then?"

She hesitates, and that tells me I've already won.

"Fine," she says, trying to play it off as if she's the one doing me a favor by letting me tag along. "I... Vanessa can get a little ahead of herself this time, so honestly, I don't know what kind of problem I'm walking in on. She's staying here at this hotel. If you're not doing anything, I could probably use your help."

"I'm not doing anything any more than you are," I say without missing a beat, pushing the door open and winking at her as she steps through. She rolls her eyes, but I could swear I see a smirk on her face from the side as she walks by with her head held high.

She's proud, confident, and quick. I had my suspicions I was dealing with a professional of some kind, and now, I'm sure of it.

We make our way down the hallway and to the elevators, then down a few floors. I follow "Naomi" all the way to one of the rooms near the end of the hall, where she quickly sends a text before knocking on the door and standing in view of the peephole. I make a point to stand back from there, peering at her thoughtfully.

Soon, I hear the sound of a door unbolting, and the room opens. A willowy wisp of a woman with long, dark, glossy hair appears in the crack of the door, looking nervously at "Naomi" for a moment before opening the door the rest of the way.

"Hadley, thank god," she breathes, and then she sees me and freezes.

"It's okay, Vanessa," Hadley says quickly while I hold back a smile at learning her real name. "He's fine, I brought him along in case you were in trouble. Is anyone here with you?"

Vanessa shakes her head, still peering at me

uneasily, but she finally steps aside to let both of us in.

"Vanessa, this is Dominick," Hadley says gently as we step inside. "Dominick, this is Vanessa, a friend of mine."

I give Vanessa a nod, but she clearly isn't sure about this whole arrangement. That confirms in my mind that she and Hadley are working together on something, but I still don't know what. More interesting and possibly concerning is the fact that it obviously isn't going well on Vanessa's end.

I close the door behind us, and as soon as we're in privacy, Vanessa makes her way further back into the room and takes a seat on the bed, subtly taking a fistful of sheets and fidgeting with them while Hadley speaks.

"Okay, so what's going on?" she asks as she steps forward. I keep my distance, standing by the door and keeping an ear out for anything unusual. "Are you okay?"

"Yeah," she says. "I... I probably shouldn't have called, I didn't mean to get you worried."

"Well, obviously I'm going to be worried," Hadley says gently, taking a seat next to Vanessa. "You sounded like hell on the phone."

"I-It was my fault," Vanessa says quickly, shaking her head. "I let something get out of hand and panicked, but he's gone now."

"He?" I ask, taking a step forward and surprising

Vanessa, despite moving slowly. She turns her body to the side, and I realize what's odd about her movements: she's hiding something.

She's hiding *two* somethings.

The first is something barely sticking out from under the bed cushions, that she covers with her legs and her dress, and I realize why she suddenly sat down. I can only see the edge of it, but it's obviously a briefcase—the kind of nondescript, still-unlatched briefcase I've seen dozens of times in my line of work.

I'd bet my career that it's full of cash. The only question is, whose cash?

The second thing I notice is her arm, which she catches me noticing. She does the smart thing and uses it in hopes of distracting me from the briefcase before I can see it. She slowly brings her forearm up and shows it to Hadley, pretending to be doing so reluctantly. Hadley's jaw drops.

There's a large bruise on her forearm, obviously caused by someone grabbing her hard, probably yanking her around for some reason.

"Vanessa…" Hadley breathes, and I can see her eyes seething with fury.

"It was just some guy from the casino," Vanessa insists, shaking her head. "I was…he felt like he was being misled, it's nothing to worry about. He's gone now, and I don't think he'll be back."

"Can you describe him for me?" I ask, testing a theory.

Immediately, I see her eyes dart to the side for just a moment, and her legs shift. They're an obvious couple of tells. If she's in league with Hadley, Vanessa is surely good at lying on most days, but whatever happened to her has left her shaken. Her guard is down. Now is the time to get any information I can from her.

"Tall, broad-shouldered, dark hair, square jaw...he wore a suit with a black tie, deep voice..."

I frown. She's describing me, along with dozens of other young men working here. Like I thought, she's lying. But who is she lying for?

"Are you sure it wasn't me?" I ask, and her face pales a little. I feel bad for testing her, but I want to see if she might be willing to give up whoever she's protecting with a little gentle pressure. I don't want to push her any farther than this.

Normally, I wouldn't be so interested in other people's secrets, but this duo has proven that they're skilled gamblers who have reason to hide large amounts of money from the kinds of men who aren't afraid to leave bruises on women. That makes it my business.

"Look, we're not escorts, if that's what you're insinuating," Hadley says quickly, realizing that she needs to come to Vanessa's side on this. I hold up a hand, nodding gently.

"Sorry. Just trying to lighten the mood a little. Listen, if someone's threatening you, I can make that problem go away. You two are obviously a pair of women with good heads on your shoulders, and I don't like the idea that someone around here thinks he can hurt one of you."

Hadley and Vanessa look at each other, and the brief glance they share is the kind of knowing look that tells me they know something important that I don't. That makes me uncomfortable, but there isn't anything I can do about it unless they're willing to divulge. And I have a feeling it has to do with whoever gave Vanessa that bruise and paid her all that money under the bed to keep her quiet about it.

Of course, I could just pull out my credentials on them and force the truth out, but Hadley intrigues me more than that. I want to see where she leads me of her own free will.

"I think I'd really just like a drink tonight," Vanessa says at last, looking at Hadley, who nods in understanding.

"We'll get room service up here," Hadley says. She then looks up at me, stands to her feet, and strides over, taking out her phone. "I don't want to make you think I'm not grateful for everything tonight."

"I can think of worse ways I've been kicked out of a hotel room," I say with a pleasant smile that seems to almost make her laugh.

"Then let's stay in touch and see if I don't kick

you out again next time," she says with meaningful, lidded eyes.

We trade numbers, and I tell them both one more time to get in touch with me if anything goes wrong tonight. I can feel both pairs of eyes on my back as I leave two women alone and close the door behind me. In the hallway, I take a deep breath before heading down the hallway.

I call up one of the other enforcers running security with me once I'm far enough away that I don't think there's a chance either of them could hear me if they wanted to.

"Tim," I say when he picks up. "What's the situation on the floor?"

"All's well. Think people noticed how you dealt with that schmuck who tried to pick a fight with the bartender and figured tonight wasn't their night."

I chuckle.

"Good, glad things don't melt down without me."

"Where you been, anyways?"

"Just following a lead. Didn't turn anything up though," I lie. "So I owe you a beer for not telling anyone I ran off on the job." That's a joke, of course. Those of us running the floor are perfectly entitled to take care of business as we see fit, and if there had been a real problem, my phone would have been blowing up with calls from the guys.

"Sure thing, overachiever," Tim chuckles. "Not like you're on thin ice or anything, so you got nothin' to worry about. Ain't no secret that Jerry likes you. That's pretty fuckin' rare."

"High praise, coming from you," I say mildly.

"He treats most of us like shit, so yea, take all the praise you want. But let's not pat ourselves on the back too much tonight," he says. "We got another problem to look into. Boss says we got cleaned out good tonight, and I mean *real* fuckin' good. Professional-good. It's gotta be a team, and he says he wants their heads on plates *yesterday*."

I stop dead in my tracks, and I'm sorely tempted to look back.

You just got a hell of a lot more interesting, Hadley.

"You there, Dom? Did that lead of yours give you any clue about what might be going on down here?"

I think for a moment before replying.

"No," I lie.

"Would you like a glass of champagne, miss?" asks one of the waiters roaming around the casino in a pressed white suit. He holds a round silver platter up nearly over his head as he bends slightly to address me. I'm sitting at a poker table, doing my damnedest to pay attention and keep my winning streak from burning out.

It's nearly seven in the evening and I still need to hit my quota. Normally, by now I might have struck that magical number and been set free to hit the casino bar and have a celebratory drink before retreating back to my hotel suite to sit in bed and order room service.

It's not that I really mind being around a lot of people. I can cope with just about any social interaction with ease. People don't make me nervous anymore, even the big shots and the annoying folks who can't keep their noses out of my business.

But at the end of a night, I usually just want to be alone. I celebrate my success alone, and I would endure my failures—if they ever happened—alone. It's just the way I function.

"No, thank you," I tell the waiter, forcing a demure smile and batting my eyelashes. "Champagne is for winners, and I'm not feeling all too confident about my hand tonight."

It's a lie. A flat-out, bald-faced lie. I am actually feeling pretty damn confident about my likelihood of utterly wiping this game. But everything I say and do is meant to accentuate and flesh out the character I'm playing at the moment.

Right now, I'm betting against two men in their late forties to early fifties. They look like new money. Like they've only been to a casino in their dreams up until now. The two of them are dressed in that overly ostentatious manner with which men who don't know how to wear wealth well get dressed. The suits are too big. They haven't learned the benefit of hiring a tailor yet. Their ties are slightly askew and too loose. They're the wide and short variety that's gone way out of style by today's standards. Their shoes are too shiny, too stiff-looking. Brand new. Probably bought here in the city.

And most importantly, both of these guys are

smirking at me like I'm an easy target. Like I'm some wispy ingenue of a woman who can hardly count to one hundred, much less count cards and do the kind of mathematical gymnastics required to wreck their spanking-new fortunes singlehandedly.

As offensive and unpalatable as it is to be regarded like a little girl who just happened to wander into a casino and get lost, I have to remind myself that this is good. This is where I want them. Because if I can convince them I don't know what I'm doing, they let their guard down. They get cocky. And cocky men make big mistakes.

Sure enough, my little fake confession to the waiter makes them both call it. I know they think they've got it in the bag—two on one? How could they lose?

But lose they do, and as I collect my winnings, I give them a dazzling smile.

"My goodness. I guess beginner's luck isn't just a myth!" I giggle as I scrape the chips into my designer handbag. "Have a lovely evening, gentlemen. It's been a real treat."

With that, I swish away from the table, leaving those gape-mouthed, mid-life crisis goons behind. I'm very nearly at my quota now. Just a little more. But annoyingly, the second I'm not fully engaged in a game, my mind wanders back to a much less helpful topic: the events of last night.

I have to admit, it's all being weighing on me pretty heavily. Vanessa is a good friend of mine, or rather, the closest alternative to a good friend a girl like me can have in this industry. We don't know each other extremely well, which is par for the course in our career path. The less you know about one another, the better. It lessens the chances of somebody slipping up and spilling all your secrets, both legal and illegal.

But I like Vanessa. She's a genuinely kind, sweet soul, and she doesn't deserve to be mistreated. Besides, if there's a guy stalking through the casino looking for women to victimize, that's bad news for all of us. Me, included.

It's why I rarely even give a man I don't know the time of day. Hell, even the men I *do* know have to work for it. I don't have space in my life for a man. Not for romancing one, anyway. I already have one great love, and it's the thrill of a win. It's the satisfaction of hearing my armful of chips clatter over the exchange counter. It's the feeling of cold hard cash in my hands.

I have yet to meet a man who can elicit the same exhilaration from me that money can.

Except... that might not be true anymore.

I have met a man who could probably compete with my love of chasing dollar signs, if I give him the chance. I woke up this morning with his face in my head. Those brown eyes smoldering with mischief and danger. His dark hair perfectly coiffed, but in a way that told me he never needed to put much effort into it. He isn't one of those guys who carries a little tube of hair gel to comb it back into some Wolf of Wall Street oil slick. And that body... I could tell exactly how powerful he was even through the clean lines and angles of his tailored suit. *That* is a man I could have some fun with. I am one-hundred-percent certain of that.

But I'm not here to play around with some startlingly good-looking stranger. I'm here to win. I'm here to get my job done so I can pay my boss and finally breathe a sigh of relief, knowing I'm in the clear once again. I'm one of his biggest earners, and my boss sees me as a cash cow.

I know that because he's told me so.

He's not exactly the most subtle or tactful guy, but when you have the kind of fortune he's accrued, the normal rules of social niceties don't apply to you anymore. However much the toll is for being a raging asshole, he can pay it. No problem. Just cut a check and saunter off with a middle finger high in the air.

That's the level of wealth and jackassery I'm dealing with here. I need to keep him happy and meet my number for the day. Happy boss, happy me. At least, that's the way it's been so far.

I know I'm his star card counter, but it's still a position I need to claw for every day. Every time I bet, there's a chance I could lose and slide back out of his good graces. I can't let that happen. Besides...the ten-percent cut of my winnings that I get to keep is important to me.

I'm saving up. I'm going to buy myself a way out of this cycle, travel the world, eat bread and cheese on some wrought-iron balcony overlooking fields of olive trees.

But for now, there's another fantasy elbowing its way in front of that usual daydream.

It's the fantasy of running into Dominick again, of bumping into his hard, strong body at the bar and following through on the night of passion we were so crudely interrupted from last night. Not that I blame Vanessa. It's not her fault someone attacked her. And all day I've been telling myself it's fate, intervening to keep me from making the big mistake of sleeping with a mysterious guy like Dom. He's just a distraction.

Besides, now that he knows I lied to him about my name, I'm sure he's too put off to want me anyway. That's the price I pay for secrecy. No one gets in.

I sit down at another table. This time, it's a group of men in their twenties. Barely old enough to slip past the bouncers. Children, really. So I don't go for the wilting violet this time. I play the femme fatale. I cross my legs so that the split up one side of my sleek black dress exposes more of my milky-white thigh. I arch my eyebrows. I don't say a word with my lips, but I dole out warnings with my eyes. Before long, I've got these kids shaking in their designer sneakers. I sweep the game and walk away far, far above my quota.

My faith in my ability to focus and win is restored. My recurring fantasies of Dominick aren't cramping my style. That's a relief. I'm flying high, my handbag clinking with chips, when I get a text message.

I check my phone, expecting it to be Vanessa. But to my surprise, it's Dom.

My heart starts to pound as I read the message.

You look divine tonight.

Before I can hammer out a response, another message appears.

Look up. Across the room. Straight ahead.

I do as I'm told, raising my eyes to stare across the crowded casino. As though a spotlight from heaven is shining on him, I immediately lock onto Dominick, who's standing at the mouth of the hallway that opens into the broad, busy room of the casino. My breath catches in my throat, my heart racing. I can feel my veins flooding with adrenaline. I feel both hot and cold at the same time and there's this magnetic, irresistible pull dragging me to him. I can't resist, and I don't want to. I'm already riding high on victory tonight. Why not cap it off with a little reward?

My legs carry me across the room as though I'm floating in mid-air. When I reach Dominick, there's nothing we have to say. We both know exactly what we want, what we're here for. He reaches for my hand and I let him take it. I lead him down the hall to the elevator. As soon the metal doors slide shut, I press the button for the fourteenth floor and then turn to kiss him on the lips. He leans into me, his broad hand sliding around to cup the back of my head. His fingers tangle in my long, red hair as his tongue probes into my mouth. I let out a little sigh, molding my body to his as the elevator ascends. I'm already getting wet. I can feel myself warming, opening, blossoming for this man.

We're going to pick up right where we left off. That's a given.

Ding.

The elevator doors part, and I lead Dom by the hand down the short hallway to my suite. I swipe the key card and the door creaks open, the two of us spilling into the room. He presses me up against the wall in the foyer, and I let out a slightly startled giggle as I reach blindly, fumbling to close the door behind us.

Dom doesn't let up. He doesn't ease into it. His hands slip down my face, his thumbs tracing the slant of my jawline, then further down over my neck, closing gently, lightly around my throat. A spiral of delight rips through my body at the soft pressure of big, powerful hands pressing against my throat. I smile against his lips, shuddering with pleasure.

Most men are too afraid to toy with me like this. They fear me.

I know what I look like. I know how intimidating I can be to lesser men. They look at me and see a woman who is untouchable, made less of flesh than marble. I'm just an object to be admired from a safe, respectful distance, never to be touched, for fear that I will shatter into a thousand pieces and cut them. That's not to say that men don't fantasize about doing to me the same thing Dominick is doing, but none of them have the cajones to follow through.

I'm not looking for a man to coddle me, though. And I sure as hell am not looking for a man to try and tame me. I just want him to regard me like the strong, thrill-seeking wild animal I really am. If we can stoke each other's fires, that's what I want. Don't let me burn out. Keep the flames licking higher and higher.

"I can't get you out of my head," Dom hisses in my ear, sending a delicious shiver down my spine. His hands slip down to my breasts, groping me through the thin black fabric of my dress. I'm not wearing a bra. It's intentional. Sometimes when I sit down at a table with a group of men, all it takes is for me to lean forward slightly, and they're all goners. The natural bounce of my ample breasts when I shift around is more than enough to keep their eyes on my chest rather than on the cards in their hands. It's just another lure to catch losers.

But Dom isn't so easily mired. He touches me with authority, like he's met my every curve before. Like he knows exactly what buttons to push to make me keen and writhe in his grasp. It's intoxicating, being held and moved with such confidence. I can tell Dom is a cautious man, but he doesn't second guess himself. He identifies what he wants, and then promptly seizes it, and god forbid anyone stand in his way.

We're more alike than I could've imagined.

His fingers roll my nipples between them, the silky fabric of my dress only heightening my pleasure. I moan, arching my back as he leans in and kisses the soft flesh of my neck, just an inch or two below my ear. His teeth graze my skin lightly, just enough to thrill me. And then he bites down gently, and the explosion of complex bliss mingled edged with just the faintest hint of pain nearly makes me collapse. But Dominick holds me up, his body pressed against me. He roughly wedges a leg between my thighs and hikes up the skirt of my gown with his free hand, gathering the folds of black fabric around my hips and exposing the expensive, black lace lingerie underneath.

"You're a woman with means," he growls. "I can see that. And I must say, I like the way you spend your money," he adds, running his fingertips along my damp slit through my designer panties. I whimper and buck against him, longing for more.

He smirks and uses a finger to deftly hook under my panties, slipping them easily to the side so that my slick folds are exposed to the air. I hold my breath as Dom slowly, rhythmically runs his fingers up and down the middle, teasing me, making me wetter by the second. When he finally slides two long fingers inside of me, I gasp and shiver. He holds me in place while his fingers slide in and out of my slick hole, crooking ever so slightly to better stroke my g-spot deep within. With every stroke, I'm getting closer and closer, my whole body tensing for a release. Usually it takes so much longer than this, even by myself. But it's like he has magical fingers. Nobody has ever touched me this way before.

"I'm so close," I murmur breathlessly.

"Good. Come for me, baby," he whispers, and I can't help but obey.

I cry out with pleasure, my pussy clenching with every shockwave of pleasure. To my surprise, Dom drops to his knees in front of me. I open my eyes to see him drape my leg over his left shoulder, keeping my dress hiked up to my hips as he leans in and begins to devour my slick, twitching cunny. I whimper and moan at the sensation of his tongue, rigidly circling my clit, lapping up every drop of my sweet honey. I instinctively reach down to run my fingers through his hair as he eats me out, seemingly ravenous for me. The thin straps of my dress slip down my shoulders and my legs begin to shake as I hurtle toward another climax.

"Oh—Dom," I choke out, just before gushing over his tongue and lips.

He groans appreciatively, and just when I think he might be done with me, I'm startled to see him stand up and scoop me into his arms. "Where are we going?" I laugh, glancing around the room. I assume he's going to lay me down on the sleek white leather sofa or the authentic Persian rug on the floor, or even just carry me off to the bedroom just off the main sitting area.

But where he actually takes me is wildly different and unexpected. Dom carries me out the glossy French doors onto the balcony before setting me down. My eyes widen and my heart starts to gallop along at a dangerous pace. This is risky and we both know it, but when Dom leans back against the railing and unbuttons his suit pants, sliding down his black boxers to let his massive, thick shaft bounce free into the night air, I can feel myself salivating in anticipation.

I can't remember the last time I ever wanted to touch someone so badly. In fact, I don't think it's ever happened before. Not like this. I lick my lips and drop to my knees in front of him, not giving a damn that the knees of my thigh-high hosiery are being frictioned into ragged holes. I might even have bruises later. I already know Dominick has kissed soft bruises into my neck. I should be more worried about this, about ruining my appearance which is so integral to my success on the casino floor. But right now, I couldn't possibly care less. All I want is to wrap my lips around that glorious cock. And so I do. I lean forward and fold my hands around his shaft, pumping gently at first, teasing the engorged head of his cock with the tip of my tongue. I swirl it around, licking and tonguing the delicate underside before Dom reaches down to press slightly at the back of my head, guiding me to take more of him.

It's what I want, too.

I moan, sending vibrations through his body as I tug his full, thick length into my mouth. I swallow him down to the root, my hands fondling his sac while the head of his cock brushes against my throat. I can feel myself getting wetter between my thighs. I love the sensation of a huge cock stretching my cheeks, poking at my throat, filling up one of my eager holes.

And the way he's sighing and groaning as I bob up and down, sucking harder and faster. I'm not usually one to offer service. I'm much more accustomed to being served. But I can't resist Dominick.

I can't resist his cock.

I want to make him feel as good as he's made me feel. His fingers tangle in my hair, pressing me down, his hips thrusting involuntarily as his cock rams into my throat. It hits me again that we're outside on the balcony. I'm no fool. I know to expect security cameras somewhere around here. Some bored security monitor guy could be watching us.

For some reason, that doesn't turn me off. In fact, it just makes the whole situation even hotter. I decide that if I'm going to be on camera, I might as well make it a damn good performance. But before I can bring Dom over the edge, he pushes me back. His cock leaves my mouth with a wet pop and I peer up at him wide-eyed, almost pouting with disappointment. But he only smirks and crooks a finger, gesturing for me to get up.

I stand up and he pulls me close, kissing me hard. It gives me a thrill to know that he's tasting himself on my lips. He doesn't shy away from it. He growls against my mouth, his hand slipping down to hike my dress up and stroke my slick pussy.

"What's your plan here, handsome?" I mumble in his ear.

"I'm going to fuck you in front of the whole strip," he replies in a rasping voice. "People come to Vegas for a show, and that's exactly what we're going to give them."

With that, he slides his leg between my thighs again, hoisting me up just enough to position the head of his cock at my slick opening. I hold my breath as he slowly pushes inside, taking me inch by inch. I moan and whimper incoherently, my body shuddering as he sheathes himself completely inside me until the tip nudges against my g-spot. Over his shoulder, I can see the city of Las Vegas far, far below. The bright neon lights. The standstill traffic. The crowds weaving down the streets like a twisted river. One misstep by Dominick could send one or both of us hurtling over the edge to a bloody death.

And yet, it's not fear that fills my heart. It's desire.

Dom thrusts faster and harder, his lips capturing mine in a passionate kiss as he fucks me, both of us gasping and moaning in the throes of unbelievable pleasure. It's the thrill of being seen. It's the threat of falling to our deaths. It's the insanity of trusting a man I hardly know to hold me and fuck me like I deserve to be. His lips trail from my mouth to my ear, and he murmurs my name, my real name. Hearing those two syllables on his lips make me shudder. He says my name with such certainty. As though to say, *of course it's you.*

"Harder," I whisper fervently, between gritted teeth.

He fucks me harder, the two of us grinding together, mostly clothed and staring feverishly into each other's eyes. His cock slams into that tantalizing place inside me again and again, our bodies moving in perfect tandem until finally, with a combined cry, we both come. I feel his cock explode with hot, sticky seed deep inside my clenching, pulsing cunny. He kisses me through the waves of pleasure, the two of us clinging together in strange desperation, far above the city.

I still feel as warm and relaxed when I wake up the next morning, every muscle in my body thanking me for what we did last night. I move my legs in my sheets until I felt her warm skin still in bed, and I have to say, I'm surprised. I would have bet anything that she'd be gone this morning, possibly with as much personal information of mine she could get her hands on. I'm a heavy sleeper, it wouldn't have been very hard.

But she's still sleeping quietly next to me, red hair strewn over her face in the darkness of the room. I can just barely make out her features, half-buried in sheets. Her eyes haven't opened yet, and I don't get the impression she's faking being asleep... but I wouldn't put it past her, either.

Slowly, I slide out of the sheets and stand up, stretch, and head over to the bathroom after grabbing my phone. The bathroom doors are pretty solid, so with the white noise of the shower water running and the fan going, it's easy to do something without being overheard.

Naturally, I call for room service and order us a lavish breakfast before jumping in the shower.

Steaming hot water washes over my naked body, relaxing every muscle even further, so much so that I feel like I could lie down and go to sleep again. I run my hands through my short, dark hair and wash out the smell of cigarette smoke and the stale air of the casino off me.

Every time the thought of that stunning redhead in bed crosses my mind, I feel my shaft start to wake up and swell, eager for another round with her. I give my cock a few strokes, letting out a soft groan as it sends ripples of warmth through my body. But with room service on the way, I don't want to spend too much time enjoying myself in the shower.

Ten minutes later, I come out feeling fresh and towel myself off before stepping outside.

As soon as the bathroom light streams out into the main room, Hadley sits bolt upright, suddenly on high alert with wide eyes and a frightened face. I freeze in place, putting a hand up and smiling warmly.

"Morning, sunshine," I say, realizing my voice is still thick with sleep. "Don't tell me I'm *that* forgettable."

She smirks, and her shoulders relax.

"Surprised to see you still here," she says smugly.

"I was thinking the same about you," I say as I stride naked into the room, watching her eyes drink in my body as she slowly pushes the sheets off herself and stretches up into the air.

Before she can reply, a knock comes at the door, and she gasps, guard going up again immediately. I wonder how used she is to this kind of lifestyle. She jumps into action-mode too quickly to be anything but experienced.

"Don't worry, that should be the room service I ordered," I say as I lazily grab my pants and pull them over my legs. As I do, she quickly grabs the nearest piece of clothing she can find, which happens to be the shirt of my suit. She slips it over her shoulders and buttons it up quickly, giving me a playful smirk as she does.

I raise an eyebrow at her, chuckling as I head to the door and pull it open. A server I recognize is standing there with the tray of breakfast foods that smell heavenly. I give him a nod, pull out a $100 bill from my back pocket to hand him, then snatch the cart inside and shut the door before he can so much as say anything.

"You work fast around here," She points out as she slides her legs out from under the sheets and props up the pillows to let her lean against the headboard while she watches me. I bring the cart over, and I start fixing a large plate for her.

The breakfast spread includes rich, applewood-smoked bacon, thick sausage patties on open-faced flaky, buttery biscuits, poached eggs seasoned with smoked paprika, and in case she was feeling like it was going to be the kind of day that called for a lot of carbs, a side of patatas bravas. To drink, I had ordered a French press full of the best coffee the house had to offer, but I also had a bottle of champagne and carafe of orange juice on the side.

"Do you like mimosas?" I ask as I hand her a heavy plate of food that makes her eyes go wide. "I'm making one for me, anyway, so…"

"Um, yeah," she says, smiling brightly. I serve us up a couple of drinks, then get onto the bed, lying opposite her with my elbow propping me up at the foot of the bed, giving us a good look at each other while we eat.

"So," I start, "you're still here, and that incident with your friend didn't scare you off—in fact, you're still raking in winnings." She watches me carefully as I speak, trying to read my face for signs of… anything. But all I wear is a curious smile, and that's all I plan on showing. "You're an intriguing woman, Hadley. Or was it Naomi?"

I have even more reason to be interested in Hadley now,

I spent all of last night wrangling with my boss

over a new problem the casino has. According to Jerry, someone cleaned us out for a few million over the past couple night. He's convinced that whoever it is is a team of professionals who must be cheating, because the odds are usually skewed to heavily in favor of the house here to let anyone get away with too much money.

But the thing is, nobody else seems to have caught onto Hadley's presence like I have. And if I were a gambling man, I'd bet that her friend Vanessa is in on the same scheme as Hadley, part of the same team. But nobody pays attention to the women. Everyone, especially the men, just assume they're wall flowers there to look pretty and go home with some rich gambler who hits a lucky break.

So, that means that by lying here, looking at nearly six feet of a gorgeous and cunning woman who's at least pretending to be this into me and doesn't seem to know who I am or who I work for... I find myself in a very interesting position.

I know Hadley is up to something, and nobody else does, not even my boss.

"I'm not apologizing for giving a fake name, if that's what you're fishing for," she says, smirking at me while sipping a mimosa. "I didn't have any idea who you were. And I still don't, to be honest, but you've exposed more of me than anyone else at this casino."

"I don't blame you," I say, picking around my

biscuit. "Cleaning out a bunch of rich fucks like them? It's a dangerous game, but you look like you know how to handle yourself. I'd be more surprised if you didn't give a fake name."

"Well, this one's real," she says. "Vanessa was... not in a great place. She's alright now, though, if you were curious."

"I'm more curious about you," I say with a wink.

"Yes, you are," she muses, narrowing her eyes at me. "That's worrisome, you know."

"What can I say? It's not every day you see someone like you walk through the doors of this place and clean house that well *without* cheating."

She arches a perfectly manicured eyebrow at me.

"And how do you know I'm playing fair?" she challenges me, tilting her head to the side.

"I think you don't need to cheat," I say simply. "You've got skill, and a lot of it, and the kinds of guys you play with don't recognize that. I bet it makes it easy to take them for a ride. I can only imagine what kind of a rush that is."

A smile curls her lips up, and I can tell I've hit on something interesting.

"You don't know the half of it," she purrs.

I was almost afraid she'd say that.

Jerry Laskin isn't the kind of guy you fuck around with. If you can't play at the big boy table, get the fuck out. So when he told me last night that I needed to find out whoever was cheating him out of that much money and put a bullet in their brain, I know he doesn't really care if the guest is actually cheating. It could be a perfectly legitimate professional gambler.

Point is, nobody beats the mafia.

Losing this much money is a big slap to the face. And he wasn't exaggerating—we lost tens of millions last night. It's definitely a team of people, and I'd be willing to bet my career that Hadley is part of that team. I just need to find out how it works…

…and then decide what to do with that valuable information.

"So, are you planning on being a tease all morning, or are you going to tell me the half of it?" I ask.

"You know what?" she says after a thoughtful sip of mimosa. "I think I will. And you know why?"

"Can't imagine," I say with a mild smile.

"Because you're the only guy I've run into in this game who isn't a complete dipshit, and I'm playing a big game," she says, crossing her legs under her and smiling deviously. She's excited, and it occurs to me that I might be the first person she's letting in on this.

Is she desperate to tell someone? Secrets can be hard to keep, surprisingly so, and especially when there's this much money involved. There's a look in her eyes I recognize. It's loneliness, but it's sparked by that wild streak she has, that thirst for adrenaline I saw so clearly out on the balcony last night.

Yeah, she's eager for someone she sees as being on her level.

"I've seen some pretty big games in my day, so you've got my attention," I say.

She gives one more moment's hesitant thought before she smiles and starts talking.

"You probably figured out Vanessa and I aren't just friends, exactly," she says. "We're sort of like coworkers. Teammates. That doe-eyed wilting flower routine didn't fool you the other night, did it? She works the tables every bit as well as I do."

I raise my eyebrows, feeling a sinking sensation in my gut. If Hadley is the one at the center of this web, I'm going to have a major problem. I show none of that emotion, though.

"You're right, we don't cheat, and you're right, it's because we don't need to," she goes on, looking smugger and prouder of herself by the moment. I can tell she has *really* been waiting a long time to be able to talk about this. I feel privileged to be the one to hear it. "The guys out there, they take one look at us and write us off. Yeah, I play up the 'dumb debutante' routine, but I barely need to. Some of the girls don't even bother with that."

"Wow, how many of you are there?" I ask.

"More than two," she says tantalizingly. "And we've been all over the world doing this. Vegas is one thing, but I've seen so much more. Montenegro, Nepal, Monaco, Tokyo, you name it. We don't hit those exclusive lakeside retreats where drug lords and arms dealers gamble with billions, though. We need places where we can blend in and draw attention all at the same time. I can barely believe this is real, sometimes. But we always clean house and are on a jet to the next place before anyone has time to do anything about it."

And that's exactly what you're about to do here.

"So, why tell me all this?" I ask, making myself vulnerable by giving her an out, but I'm liking what I'm hearing more by the minute. "I could ruin everything for you, couldn't I?"

"Who'd believe you?" she replies, and I see the flare of excitement in her eyes. "That's the best and worst part—you're not the first guy I've told about this." I stare, surprised, but her face is grinning. "You're the first to actually listen, but I've flirted with guys before. How could I not? You'd do the same if you were in my shoes."

I have to admit, she's right, and I nod.

"But your next question is, why put the whole thing at risk for that?" She sets her now-empty plate aside and lays on her stomach, crossing her legs at the ankles behind her and perching her chin on her folded hands and smiling at me. "It's because of our boss."

Alarm bells go off in my head, and I tilt my head to the side. *Now* I'm getting somewhere.

"So, this isn't an independent thing?" I ask.

"I wish," she says, shaking her head. "No, Carl—oh, excuse me, *Mr. Owens* as he insists on being called—takes most of the cut. By a big margin. Basically, he's our overhead. He's some pervy old rich heir who has nothing better to do with his life than organize a team of young and lovely gamblers, like *moi*," she says with a flutter of her eyelashes, "and he flies us around the world to clean house with him."

I raise my eyebrows as everything clicks in my head.

So, Carl Owens is the man responsible for cleaning out a mafia casino for millions of dollars in winnings, all by pulling the strings with a team of beautiful women who don't even have to cheat to get what they want. Astounding.

"That's a hell of a plan," I admit, looking appropriately stunned in such a way that she seems satisfied with my reaction.

"Right? It would be perfect, if only he was thoughtful enough to pay us enough."

"What's your cut?"

"Fucking 10%," she says, frowning ruefully. "Sure, that's a lot of money, but compared to what he's raking in for doing nothing but getting handsy with us and coaching us on things we already know? It's an insult."

"It really is," I say, furrowing my eyebrows. That cut would be outrageous even by mafia standards, especially considering the risk involved.

The smile has faded from my face by a bit, because now, I have a lot to think about and not much time to figure out how to handle it.

It should be simple. I now have the name of the man who's ripping the mob off, and I have Hadley. If Hadley had any idea how deep in the mafia I am, she wouldn't be singing like a canary for me right now. If she knew I'm one job away from becoming a made man, she'd be a little more protective of her boss. But then again, she doesn't seem to have any love for Carl, and he sounds like a piece of shit. She, on the other hand, is not a piece of shit. Hell, right now, she's the most interesting woman I've met in my life, and I want to know more.

But if I did my job right, she'd be on the chopping block right along with Vanessa and Carl Owens. And that's the big question I'm faced with: do I want to be a good mobster and do the job that's expected of me?

Or do I let them get away with it and pretend I didn't see anything?

Hadley deserves something good, better than what she's getting now. Vanessa and the other girls probably deserve the same, if Hadley is telling the truth.

I'm holding the cards now, and I get to decide who wins.

But I'm sensing a third option, and it's increasingly interesting.

"So, why don't the lot of you just ditch Carl and

go on your own?" I ask, smiling, and the question seems to delight her.

"I like how you think, but Carl is the glue keeping the operation together right now," she admits. "Plenty of the girls are at least content with what we're doing, not enough to rebel against him. He's got a kind of... intimidating force of personality." I hate him already. "And besides, he has the jet, he has the professionals who make all this happen," she says, gesturing to her face. She's still got most of her makeup on from last night.

I nod, but now I'm thinking. The amount of money they made last night would be more than enough to get things started off on their own. I wonder if they've made the handoff to Carl yet...

But just as that thought crosses my mind, I get a text. I check it, and see it's from Jerry, telling me to call him immediately. I have to get back to my regular duties, or I'll look suspicious. In a hurry, I stand up and buckle my belt.

"Where are you going?" she asks, crestfallen.

"Got to go," I say brusquely, reaching my hand out. "And I'll need that shirt back."

I can see the disappointment and frustration melting over her face, and it's heartbreaking, but I can't linger any longer than this. She tears the shirt off her shoulders and thrusts it at me with a scowl.

"Fine, whatever," she scoffs, standing up and heading to the bathroom. "Figures."

I watch her go as I button my shirt back on. I'll have to make it up to her somehow, but for now, I need to collect my thoughts. I head out the room once I'm dressed, and as I go, I already have a plan hatching in my head.

It's simple and brutal, two things that go a long way in the mafia.

If I kill Hadley's boss, then she gets to keep the money she earned, and I get to advance in the mafia. Nobody knows the girls are involved, and they disappear without a trace.

It's perfect.

"Vodka cranberry, please," I murmur softly to Antonio the bartender, leaning on the bar counter with my elbow. "And make it a double. Might as well."

"Double your pleasure, got it," he replies, without an ounce of flirtation.

I smile faintly, glad that at least one man in this place still has a sense of humor. All evening, it's been one rotten egg after another. Men who ogle me. Men who look down at me. Men who beg to know my name and where I'm from and what my room number is, as if there's an ice cube's chance in hell I would ever give any of them the time of day.

The most annoying part, by far, though is the fact that they keep beating me.

Well, scratch that. They don't win because they're better at the game, at card counting, than I am. They have been winning purely because I'm not doing my ultimate best.

It's not for lack of trying, either. I've been doing everything in my power to direct my mind toward something useful, something that will earn my paycheck. I need to focus. I need to be on my A-game and wipe the casino floor with these chumps.

Normally, this would be a victorious day for me. I had the best sex of my life last night, and I doubt I will ever experience any sexual encounter quite so satisfying or exciting. It still brings a smile to my lips to think of the way Dominick leaned back against that railing, the only thing separating us from a freefall to hell a wrought-iron balustrade that probably hasn't been inspected for safety in a decade.

I have done something risky things in my time on this planet. I went hiking alone in the Patagonian wilderness in winter. I skied in Switzerland, skipping the bunny slopes and heading straight to the big leagues, my body buzzing with liquor and a thirst to prove myself. I wandered the streets of Fez by myself, dodging aggressive street merchants and hungry-eyed men who looked at me like an easy target.

Hell, the way I make my money is risky. I'm always on the edge, and I thought nothing could surprise me anymore. But Dominick surprised me. He showed me a wildness I haven't tapped into in a long, long time.

And then he had to go and ruin it all.

It's as though my beautiful night was the result of some magical wish on a timer. In the morning my carriage turned back into a pumpkin and my prince charming transformed into just your everyday, garden-variety prick.

I still can't believe how rude he sounded when he demanded his shirt back from me. As if I was going to steal it and sell it on the internet or something. It's a shirt. Who cares? Besides, what kind of business could he possibly have had to tend to that was more important than lounging in bed with me eating room service breakfast and enjoying each other's company?

I don't take well to being treated so brusquely. I'm a once-in-a-lifetime catch, and I'll be damned if I let any man knock me off-kilter. It's not pride that makes me this way. It's self-preservation, through and through. If I protect my heart, if I filter out the vast majority of men, it's less likely that I'll get hurt or distracted. In my line of work, distraction can be deadly. I have sharpened my abilities to tune out anyone who threatens my focus.

I guess I still have some work left to do, though, because Dominick has been crowding my thoughts ever since he left my hotel suite this morning so abruptly.

My phone buzzes and my heart skips a beat as I whip it out to check for a text message, half-expecting it to be some sort of apology from Dom. But no such luck. It's from my coworker, probably urged to text me by my boss. Carl likes to contract out his work. Even in small ways. I know this message is really from him.

I instantly want to scold myself for being so excited by the idea of Dominick reaching out to me. He's lost his chance. I have to keep it that way.

The message from my colleague reads: *How's that 1m from last night treating you?*

I sigh and roll my eyes, feeling my stomach twist up into anxious knots. It takes a lot to make me nervous, but when I see the digital time on my cell phone screen, I can't help but feel a twinge of worry. It's nearly ten at night. Two hours to midnight and I've managed to squander away half last night's winnings, which I was supposed to invest into an even bigger payout, as per my instructions from the boss man.

When I met him for a brief, light lunch in the hotel restaurant at noon today, he informed me of how pleased he was with my progress. The million I won yesterday was meant to be planted like a seed. To grow and multiply, making him an even wealthier man. That's how he is. Never, ever satisfied. I suppose he's not unlike any gambler in that way. No payout is enough. It's always just a stepping stone to greater heights of wealth and luxury. And I'm the best employee. After all, he helped train me himself. I learned my basic tricks from him, although I'd like to think I've put my own spin on things. I'm a great counter, a fantastic gambler in my own right. And the boss just sees me as an extension of himself. I never fail him. I'm the most reliable cash cow he's got, so he doesn't think twice about asking me to double my winnings. Most of the time, I could do it, too.

Today, though, I'm in a funk. I curse myself inwardly for letting Dominick get into my head and dislodge all the focus and drive I've cultivated over the years. I never should have let him touch me like that. I'm smarter than this. Or at least I thought I was.

Of course, it doesn't help that I can feel the scrutinizing gaze of the bouncers and enforcers following me from table to table. When the boss told me to keep playing today, I very nearly protested the idea. I mean, we've been here long enough. Too long, in fact. The only way our system works is if we get the hell out of dodge once we've won. You can't just keep scamming the same establishment out of their money. Nobody is *this* lucky by nature. Suspicions arise. You shift from honored guest to bothersome pest. Eventually, someone is going to ask questions. Eventually, you're going to get caught.

I don't want to get dragged out of here by some stodgy security guard. It's not good for my brand. It's not good for my reputation. And besides, the boss man has dropped team members in the past a thousand times before. Once he decides you're nothing but dead weight, you're mutinied. You're out. Dropped like a hot potato, abandoned into whatever boring, empty, low-class life he scooped you out of to begin with.

I refuse to go back. There is only moving forward for me. So despite my worries and my distraction, I have to make this money back.

I take my drink from Antonio and turn to walk back to one of the poker tables when suddenly, something catches my eye from across the room. I do a double take as my eyes fall over Dominick himself. I scowl at the sight of him, and then I realize he's engrossed in some kind of hushed, conspiratorial conversation with another man.

The other guy looks rough around the edges, despite his flashy suit. There's a beastly look in his beady black eyes, and the purplish bags under them hints at his nighttime prowler status. He clearly isn't a daytime kind of guy. He's like a predator, the kind you might run across walking alone in the deep, dark woods in a nightmare. He's burly and broad-shouldered, hinting at a body accustomed to hard labor and hard living. He's not as tall nor anywhere near as elegant as Dominick, who looks every bit as debonair and delectable as he did the first time I saw him.

Every fiber in my body longs to get closer to him,

like he's reeling me in on a fishing line without even trying. There's this magnetic pull between us that is so powerful it nearly knocks me off my feet. But so far, he hasn't seemed to notice I'm around. That's for the best, I tell my disappointed heart. He's already proven himself an unworthy object for my affection by the way he snapped at me this morning. I don't put up with stuff like that. Not for anyone. Not even for a guy like Dom.

Taking advantage of the fact that he hasn't noticed me yet, I begin to slowly and subtly work my way across the casino, inching closer and closer to their clandestine conversation. They don't look my way, but I freeze up when I see the rougher looking guy put a hand on Dominick's shoulder and guide him into a little alcove where the bachelor parties often gather to sit on leather couches and order trays of martinis while they get more and more wasted. I move along close to the wall, keeping out of sight as I wiggle up to the corner. I can't see them, and they definitely can't see me, but I can just faintly make out snippets of their conversation.

"Owens," grunts the rough guy. "Carl Owens. That's a name I never thought I'd hear in this town again."

I have to clap a hand over my mouth to keep from gasping. Did Dom just use me to get my boss's name? If the casino is onto us, then that must mean the rest of the dominoes will go tumbling down any time now.

Including me. I'm one of those dominoes. If Carl goes down, you'd better believe he will drag every one of us down with him.

"You spotted any of his little minions yet?" the rough man asks.

"Possibly," answers Dom. "Most likely. I have a few suspicions."

"Suspicion isn't good enough. I need to know for sure he's got these kids counting," is the gruff reply. "What was the name of that girl you mentioned before?"

I hold my breath, waiting to hear my name.

"Alisson," Dom says smoothly.

There's no Alisson on our team. He could have offered up my name, or Vanessa's, but he didn't.

But he still gave up my boss, and that's almost as bad. If I get caught counting to the extent that I have been, it's all over for me. My reputation, so carefully and painstakingly built, will crumble underneath my feet. I won't be able to get in anywhere. I have a very distinctive look. I'll have to change everything in order to keep going, sacrifice who I am, the version of myself I have cultivated over the years.

My fears are solidified when I hear the rough guy, who I'm starting to strongly suspect as a mafia member, asks, "Is everything still good to go for the meeting?"

"Yes. It's all falling into place as we expected. They won't be leaving with all that cash," Dominick says darkly.

"Shit," I swear to myself under my breath. I decide right then and there that if they want to play games, I won't let them take me so easily. Not without sweeping this whole place before they take me. I have heard enough of their sneaky conversation. I'm done.

I down my vodka cranberry, ordered in a rare moment of vulnerability, and stride back to the blackjack table. I delicately muscle my way through the clamoring crowds of bejeweled onlookers and take a seat. My competition, a group of men who look like high rollers, all stare at me open-mouthed. I smile. They weren't expecting the likes of me.

Neither was the dealer by the look on her face.

"Hit me," I tell her confidently.

I don't know if it's the liquor, the resentment, or the sense of impending doom hot on my heels, but something has restored my mojo. I utterly wreck the competition, leaving them red-faced and sour. I gather my chips up and move on to the next set. I flit from one game to the next, leaving a trail of devastation in my wake. I'm earning back my deficit and more. I'm flying through the ranks. And all along, I can feel a pair of blazing brown eyes on me, following me as I destroy the casino floor.

Dominick. He's watching me. The mafia guy is

gone, but Dom stays, hovering always just out of reach, watching me nearly double my money, playing into the wee hours of the morning. Around 2 AM he catches me in between tables and lays a hand on my arm. I look down at it disdainfully, then back up to glare into his face with as much venom as I can muster.

"Stop while you're ahead," he hisses, those eyes flitting around suspiciously.

"Sorry, I don't take orders outside the bedroom," I answer deftly, and sidestep him on my way to the next game, my heart thudding painfully in my chest.

Not even these gigantic designer sunglasses can block out the blazing bright desert sun over Fremont Street. I lean back in my chair, seated at two square, blocky wooden tables pushed together to be big enough to seat my team of colleagues. There are five of us here, perched in front of our respective bellinis and mimosas and various sworn-by hangover cures.

I, for one, do not like to ever admit when I'm hungover. Or under the weather. Or upset. I just like to keep my weaknesses to myself, thank you very much. But after my long night of gambling and pounding back vodka cranberries into the wee hours of the morning, there's no way to really hide how awful I feel.

My stomach is churning, my limbs feel heavy. My head is pounding as though there's a tiny man inside my brain just swinging away with a pickaxe. And I know if I were to lower my shades for even a second, my colleagues would all see the shadowy bags under my eyes, definitive proof that I'm not feeling my tip-top best.

I don't like to be vulnerable. I don't like people to know when or how to take advantage of me. Even in little ways. Nobody is allowed to get the upper hand over me. So maybe I look a little rude wearing my shades at a restaurant, but in my defense, we *are* seated outside on the back patio. So the sun is technically *right* there. And these sunglasses are expensive. Flashy. Yet another status symbol collected into my wardrobe.

It's my favorite and subtle way to tell people not to mess with me. I want my look at all times to clearly broadcast the message: *you can't afford what it costs to talk to me*. Is that harsh? Oh yes. Certainly. But in my line of work, the less conversation you have to share with strangers, the safer you are. People are always trying to understand me. Get in my head. Find out my secret. But I keep my armor tight and gleaming.

Nobody gets in.

Well, except for Dominick, I remind myself bitterly. As I sip my peach bellini, I can't help but think of him. He's weaseled his way into my thoughts, and it's driving me wild. I keep picturing the way he looked at me, the way his hand felt, heavy on my shoulder, as he gave me that hushed, fervent warning. A warning I completely refused to heed.

For better or for worse, I'm deep in this work.

This "scam," if you're honest enough to call it that.

Admittedly, I haven't spent a lot of my time on this planet being especially honest. Maybe when I was a little girl. I had a normal childhood for the most part. Both of my parents have always been supportive, always loving me no matter what risky path I journey down. I know they worry about me. They know I'm a big-time gambler, a poker player rising up through the international ranks. It's the fame they're afraid of. Maybe they think I'm going to be some kind of celebrity, unable to leave my home without being assaulted by paparazzi with gigantic cameras in my face. But what they don't understand is how cautious I am. I'm constantly outrunning my fame. It trails after me, but I've usually already moved on to the next shakedown by the time people realize who I am.

I have a distinctive look. It's intentional. But not to make myself memorable. In fact, it is my greatest hope that my competitors will forget me as soon as I leave the table. I have a reputation, but I'm done everything my power to make it a quiet one. The kind of notoriety people whisper about but don't print in the papers.

It's why I try not to have long conversations with

people I'm not already affiliated with. It's why sharing my life story with a guy like Dominick is dangerous and why I don't ever let myself do it. I'm still so disappointed in myself for giving in to his charms so easily. He really led me astray. Even one night in his arms has been enough to shake me to my core. Usually it's easy for me to control my thoughts. I have a razor-sharp focus. It's one of my greatest strengths in my career.

But Dominick has infiltrated my thoughts like some kind of super-handsome parasite, and I'm bitter about it.

This is no time for distraction, especially now that I'm sitting here commiserating with my coworkers. Or, more accurately, my assorted partners-in-crime. Apart from myself, there are two women and two men at the table, the oldest of us only thirty-four. Carl calls us his kids sometimes, which I find pretty hilarious. I guess in *some* ways he's like a father. He's domineering and authoritative and always pushing us out of our comfort zones… for money. But it's not like any of us can go running to him for comfort. He's not *that* kind of father figure. If you fuck up, you sure as hell don't expect sympathy from Carl Owens.

"Man, I'm so groggy this morning," gripes one of my colleagues, the eldest one. He's a tall, skinny former MIT nerd named Kyle. He was recruited by Carl once he got caught writing fellow students' work for them and was promptly kicked out of the prestigious university. He was the first one to join the team. Kyle is sort of the team OG, and often functions as Carl's right-hand man. He's the one who texts us what some might call "passive-aggressively encouraging" messages to keep us on our toes. When Carl's not around, he's an affable guy. But when the boss is nearby, Kyle turns right back into a raging sycophant. It's almost embarrassing.

"Yeah, I feel like I got hit by a bus last night or something," sighs the young woman seated to my left. I'm at the head of the table, purely because I showed up late, after everyone else was already seated. On my left is Monique, a stunning girl with long box braids and the brightest, most disarming smile I've ever seen outside of a toothpaste commercial. At only twenty-one, she's the baby of the group, and grew up very sheltered. Apparently, she learned how to play poker while away at Bible camp as a teenager, which I find positively delightful. She's a relatively new recruit, but she shows major promise.

The guy on my right is a quiet guy named Jasper. Well, that's the name he gave us when Carl brought him into the fold. I don't think it's his real name. I don't know his age or anything, but he looks to be around my age, give or take. Carl recruited him from some big corporate office in Hong Kong, choked by smog and hyper competition. Jasper was bored out of his mind in his big, airy high-rise office, and even though he was apparently raking in the millions, he longed for a more adventurous lifestyle.

Enter Carl Owens.

On a business trip to an underground poker tournament in the city, Carl found Jasper winning round after round with this flat, emotionless look on his face. Jasper uses the stereotypical poker face strategy. Smooth, unaffected, never intimidated. I admire him a lot. He shares little about himself, not even with us, his own colleagues. It takes a lot of willpower to be that closed-off.

And on the other side of Jasper sits a woman named Casey. She's a twenty-five-year-old spitfire with a shock of white-blonde curls that frame a round, innocent-looking face. Freckles splatter over the bridge of her button nose and her big powder-blue eyes tend to charm her competitors into a false sense of security.

Despite her angelic appearance, she's the one you really need to watch out for.

When she gets pissed, you'd better get out of her way. Casey is what you might call a wild card. She's constantly on Carl's shit list because she often has difficulty remaining calm when she loses money. Granted, she's also been blessed with the best luck I've ever seen. I've watched Casey start an evening in a fifty-thousand-dollar deficit, only to end with half a mil in her pocket. I'm pretty sure Casey is the sole reason why Carl's hair has been going white more quickly over the past two years. She's a trouble-maker, but she's got a good heart. I hesitate to say that about anyone, but with Casey it's the truth.

There are two seats still markedly unoccupied at our table, meant for Carl himself and, of course, Vanessa. She's the sweetheart of the group, but she's also a little... well, a little scatterbrained. Carl worries about Casey, but it's Vanessa who weighs on my mind. Especially right now, since her absence is burning a hole in my thoughts. After how I left her the other night, I've been worried about her, but this job doesn't leave much down time. Especially since I spent so much of yesterday deep in the hole. And besides, I try not to make a habit of being anyone's guardian. As much as I adore my teammates and genuinely enjoy their camaraderie, I still have to keep a reasonable distance. For my sake. For the sake of my fortune. And for their sake too.

"Where's Nessa?" Casey asks as if she can read my mind.

"I haven't heard from her in days," Jasper says.

"I wish I knew," I answer. "I've called her a few times and it just goes to voicemail, and she isn't replying to my texts. My guess she's either having the worst or best time of her life, and either way she wants to keep it on the downlow."

"Well, she needs to at least check in with me or the boss," Kyle says, always the deputy.

"Do you think something might have... *happened*

to her?" Monique asks in a hushed voice, her brown eyes wide.

"Here," I say, pulling out my cell phone, "I'll give her another call." Everyone watches me as I dial her number and press the phone to my ear. I listen to the line ring once, twice, three times, and so on until her voicemail kicks in.

"Hi, you've reached Vanessa—" *click*. I set the phone down and sigh.

"Nothing?" Monique prompts me, worried.

"Nothing. Just voicemail again. I've already left her several messages," I admit.

"She'll turn up. It's likely just the big city capturing her attention," Kyle says confidently. "Can we all agree to keep a look out for her, though? I mean, the boss hasn't been around much lately either, but it's normal for him to disappear. Vanessa, though, she usually checks in if she's going to flake."

"Yeah, we're all each other has in this world," Casey points out honestly.

Monique nods. "You don't think she got in a fight with Carl or anything, right?"

"No. She's too smart to take that risk," Jasper says sagely.

"Weird that Carl would miss out on a chance to day drink," Casey says, totally deadpan as she spikes her mimosa with something from her pink, sparkly flask. "And eat breakfast food. One time on a flight I watched that man order two bagels in a row."

Monique snorts. "Well, Carl's a man who knows what he wants out of life, at least."

"Yeah, cold cash and cheap breakfast foods," adds Kyle, grinning. Then he looks down the table at me. "Anyway, I wanted to congratulate you on your winning streak lately, Hadley."

"Your whole 'hapless ingenue' tactic has been working very well," Jasper says. "It's a good way to surprise your opponents into trusting you."

"Ooh yes, I heard you were killin' it," chimes Casey.

I nod slowly. "Should have won more, though," I sigh.

Jasper frowns. "Why more? Is something distracting you?"

I'm grateful for my gigantic sunglasses because they're helping to hide the pinkish blush spreading across my face at his question. I can feel the word vomit bubbling up inside me. I can only keep stuff to myself for so long before it just… comes out. And if I can't trust these guys with a tiny, stupid little secret, then who can I trust?

"Oh, you *are* distracted," Monique gasps, getting excited. "Is it about a boy?"

"A boy?" I repeat disdainfully, raising an eyebrow. "I don't get distracted by boys. But a man, now that's something else."

"What's he look like?" Casey asks, biting her lip.

"Oh, you know. The usual tall, dark, and hand-some combination," I tell her vaguely.

"What's his name?" Monique presses me.

"Bond, James Bond, from the sound of it," Casey teases.

"His name isn't important," I cut in. "We just had a very good night together and—"

"Ooooh, did you, now?" Casey giggles. Monique lets out a peal of laughter and has to clap her hands over her mouth.

"Guys, come on, we're not in seventh grade," Kyle sighs, rolling his eyes.

"Anyway. It was good. It was fun. And then in the morning, he turned back into an asshole, so it doesn't matter," I explain hastily. "I just hope I don't run into him again."

"Oh yeah, he sounds like a jerk," Monique says, giving me a pitying smile.

"Just your run-of-the-mill asshole. Just like all of them are," Casey adds. "You're better off without him. Don't let some loser throw you off your game. Men are intimidated by woman like you. It's a good thing."

"Well, I wouldn't call him a *loser*," I reply, unable to stop myself.

"Really? Because he sure sounds like one," Monique inserts.

Casey nods vigorously as the two guys at the table exchange mildly offended expressions. They know better than to interject themselves into this particular topic.

"No, he really... he wasn't that bad. I guess I'm just disappointed, that's all. I shouldn't have gotten my hopes up. That's my fault. Not his," I ramble, feeling dumber by the second.

Why am I defending him? Why do I care? What's wrong with me? He's the one who left. *He's* the one who is in the process of selling us out. I tap my foot anxiously. I need to tell Carl something, anything to get him out of this fucking town, and that's not a conversation I can have on the phone. Why isn't he here yet?

I quickly change the conversation topic, and before long, I've got them all sharing tactics and comparing strategies instead of discussing my love life or lack thereof. I listen half-heartedly as they talk about poker faces and fake-outs and what to wear and how to speak or whether to speak at all. They talk money. They talk winning and losing. And all along, my mind is far away, somewhere else completely. I cycle through three questions again and again.

Where is Carl?

Where is Vanessa?

And why, when I think of Dom, am I feeling warm and fuzzy instead of the burning rage I *should* feel?

Finally, when we've all eaten our fill of bacon,

french toast, chilaquiles, and various forms of morning-appropriate booze, the checks come. We each pay our tab and leave handsome tips, as is our ritual. When we split up to go our separate ways, I head to the sidewalk out front to try and hail a cab. But just before I can lift my arm to hail one, my phone starts buzzing in my purse. I yank it out and answer without even glancing at the caller ID on the screen.

"Hello?" I answer rather brusquely.

"Hadley! It-it's me! Please, you have to help me," hisses the petrified voice of Vanessa. My heart sinks. She sounds even more afraid than she did the other night.

"Vanessa? Oh god, what's wrong, hon? What's going on?" I ask, curling my hand over the phone so I can speak more softly into it. I step away from the curb and duck away into a narrow, dark alley to talk to her. The line is popping and snapping, an underlying crackle telling me our connection probably isn't super clear.

"Hadley—I—they got—I'm here," she croaks out between blips of static.

"Where? Where are you? Who's got you?" I demand to know.

"I don't—kidnapped—"

My eyes widen. "What? You've been kidnapped? Are you serious? Holy shit. Vanessa, listen to me. What you have to do is obey them. Do what they say, alright? Be polite. Don't give them any more reason to hurt you. Try to bond with them. And if you see a way to escape, take it. Don't hesitate. But you've got to be sure, okay?" I tell her quickly, adrenaline flooding my veins as I picture her in tears, chained up in some creep's basement.

"Hadley, the mafia—" she says frantically. The line drops out for a second and comes back when she says, "Carl—made a deal—"

"Carl? What? Carl is behind this?" I whisper, totally stunned.

"Help me, I—" Vanessa bursts out tearfully, and then the line goes dead. I stare at the phone in disbelief.

"No. No, no, no," I mutter, trying to redial the number. But it's a blocked number. No way to call it back. Someone's got Vanessa. She's in trouble, and it could be all Carl's doing.

"One more time," says Jerry Laskin, reclining in his large leather armchair, cigarette burning between his fingers as he stares at me across the casino lounge with hawkish eyes. "Start to finish."

"I get the clean gun from Marco at his place," I say as I stand by the window, letting the light behind me cast a shadow over my figure. "My target is Carl Owens, who owns a house out in the desert where he's most likely staying at while his girls do the leg work here at the casino. I've got the coordinates memorized, and my GPS is going to get me there today. I break in, find Carl, and put a bullet in his head. I leave the body, because we're sending a message. We've got people in the media ready to run the story that Carl was organizing a scam at the casinos, so it scares off anyone else thinking about pulling the same kind of shit. I drop the gun off with Marco, come back here, and run another night of security like nothing happened."

"Good," says Jerry, standing up and taking one last drag of his cigarette before putting it out in the ashtray in front of him. "And any money you find at that place is ours, so don't fucking touch it. You'll get your cut *after* our guys come in and clean up."

Jerry Laskin is the kind of man who doesn't need to spread rumors about himself. They're all true. I've seen him kill men for failing to follow his orders exactly, even ones who have been on his good side for years. His enemies don't last long, and he doesn't have a scrap of remorse in his body.

The raw recruits like to say he traded his soul to the devil so he could sleep with a clear conscience for all the things he's done.

Me, I don't give a shit.

He's a paycheck, and a good one. I make fast money and live a fast life on his dime as long as I keep breaking kneecaps when he tells me to and threatening anyone who dares fuck with us. I'm good at my job, and he rewards that. So far, that's been a good relationship between us. He thinks I'm simple. I'm ex-military, good at taking orders. In his eyes, I'm almost too good to be true.

And that's why I'm pretty damn careful about showing my strengths.

"He might not be alone at the house," I say. "What do you want done about that?"

"You're sending a message," Jerry says. "Do what you gotta do. Don't make it a bloodbath if he's got a party or some shit, but nobody's gonna mourn a few dead broads he's got lying around. One or two terrified witnesses is good, though, so don't clean the place out if there's someone to give the cops a story. Just make sure they don't get a good look at you. I'm not covering your ass if you slip up and lead the cops here."

"Understood," I say.

"Now, listen, Dom," he says, putting a hand on my shoulder and looking at me with deadly seriousness. "This is a hell of a lot more than just some fuck trying to rip us off. This is a slap to the face that money's not gonna make up for. I don't care if he waves the Hope fucking Diamond under your nose, his ass is dead, do we understand each other? Make this pig bleed. Pick him apart piece by piece, and when he squeals—because he *will*—you take that as a bonus. He'll try to promise you all the pussy you could want and more money than you'd know what to do with, but he'd put a bullet in your back the second you turn it. Me, you know how much I'm paying you, and if you get this done, consider yourself a made man. We clear?"

"Crystal."

"Good man," he says, patting me on the shoulder

and turning around to stalk back to his chair. "Now, go make me a *happy* man."

I leave the lounge and head through the casino, rolling my shoulders back and heading down to the garage to my black Aston Martin.

When I told Jerry who was behind this whole deal, he got a hell of a lot more interested in it. The name Carl Owens made Jerry's eyes practically turn red. Turns out, Carl has debts to Jerry—really, really big debts. So big that I'd be willing to bet he took out a loan from Jerry to get this wild gambling scheme going, and he's been digging himself out of debt and compounding interest ever since. The debt has grown so big and gone on so long that Jerry isn't willing to take money anymore.

Jerry wants Carl's blood. I'm going to be the smoking gun that makes that happen.

Of course, that puts me at risk in a big way. If I'm the one pulling the trigger, then I know damn well Jerry won't cover for me if the cops come after me. The only silver lining is that Jerry hates Carl so fucking much that he doesn't give a shit about the girls. At least, he doesn't seem to.

I pull the car out of the garage and take off.

I'm pissed at myself for how things have gone. This is a thicker web of murder than I was planning on getting tied up in, and I don't like surprises. I especially don't like that Hadley has been scarce recently.

If today goes well, I have a simple plan.

I kill her boss, I take her to dinner, we hash things out, I apologize for dashing out the other morning after spending the night together, and we see where things go from there. I never thought I'd be offering up a dead boss as an apology, but here I am, driving out to the desert to put a bullet in someone's head.

This is a first for me. I've broken dozens of kneecaps and interrogated endless gamblers who've tried to cheat us. Put me in a room with a man and give me a few minutes, and I'll have him spilling every secret he has.

But I've never killed.

I don't have any reservations about it. Carl Owens isn't the kind of man who's making the world a better place. He won't be missed, and unless he makes a damn convincing case when he's on his knees in front of my gun, I have a feeling he won't be dripping with enough charisma to make me second-guess myself. Still, it's a line to cross. I can tell Jerry has plans for me, and those plans involve a lot more bloodshed.

I'm on the verge of crossing the line from enforcer to hitman.

That would mean a lot more money, a lot more freedom, and a lot more respect in the mafia. Those are all good things, except for one problem.

Hadley.

I haven't stopped thinking about her since I left her room. My body still remembers how she felt, the smell of her hair, the taste of her tongue. I've never felt this way about someone before, but fuck, she left one hell of an impression on me. It's not just her beauty that attracts me. It's her mind.

She's a genius, plain and simple. We both have the combo of mathematical minds and pure ambition that I never see in other people. She likes playing mind games with people, and I can tell that this gig she's tied up in is the biggest rush she's enjoyed in her life. She thrives on this shit. I would too. She has a spark that not even the other girls have.

She's special in a way I never expected to encounter.

And that's just one huge goddamn distraction to me.

While I'm driving, I call up Marco and listen to ring after ring. Finally, a groggy voice answers the phone.

"What?"

"Marco? This is Dom, where are you?"

"Dom? What the...ah, shit," he groans, and I clench my jaw.

"What's the problem, Marco? Where the fuck are you? We have a handoff to make."

"I uh...got a little carried away at the clubs last night. I... might not be in Vegas right now."

"Fucking- where the fuck are you, Marco?"

"Well, I never really got around to driving home from LA last night like I meant to."

I cut the call without saying another word to him. I swear to god, I could kill him with my own hands next time I see him.

It doesn't matter. I'll take care of Carl with the knife I have strapped to my leg. I like having more control over the kill, anyway. I don't plan on getting too fancy. He isn't expecting me. That gives me the biggest advantage I could hope for. I'm going to get in and get out in under an hour, ideally.

When I pull up to the manor, I'm not surprised by what I see. It isn't exactly a palatial villa, but it's a damn nice little hideaway for weeks he probably spends raking in money from the Vegas casinos. His main estate is probably somewhere else, maybe not even in the US, but a guy like Carl Owens must know the value of not staying in one place too long. This is how he built his tiny little empire.

I can't help but wonder what the sex workers in the city think about this address.

Out here, there really isn't any way to approach a place without being seen, so I rely on speed instead. I know I'm going to have to move fast. I bring my vehicle to a stop and I climb out of my car, rolling my shoulders back.

I make my way around the back of the house in case he saw me pull up, and I get low against the wall, pulling out my knife. I check in a few windows as I move, and I see lights on inside, but no movement.

This manor isn't just a little hideaway for Carl. It was a gift from the mafia when he started borrowing money. The mob likes to do that kind of thing so they keep their investments close and keep an eye on them. The fact that Carl's here proves that he doesn't think we're onto him. That's ideal.

Around the back are two sweeping staircases leading up to a balcony, which offers a gorgeous view of the inground pool. I can practically hear and smell the house parties that have been held here, probably with wealthy business associates lusting after the very women who are doing the leg work for this scheme of Carl's.

Up on that balcony is a sliding glass door that's partially open. Someone has come through it recently.

Holding the knife close, I make my way up the stairs to the balcony, ready for anything. If I have to throw the knife, then by god, I'll do it. I'm not about to let this job slip out from under me.

When I get to the glass doors, my neck hairs stand on end when I hear the sound of footsteps approaching. I quickly move up against the wall next to the door and press my body against it, breathing very slowly and silently, watching the opening. All it'll take is for him to walk through those doors.

When the footsteps are just around the corner, my muscles are poised to strike.

And a moment later, I'm paralyzed with surprise when Hadley strolls through the door.

She's hard to recognize in such a casual outfit—simple jeans, a t-shirt, glasses, and her hair pulled back in a loose ponytail that somehow all makes her look just as beautiful as when she's dressed up elaborately. My eyes get drawn to her ass immediately as she walks by me without so much as noticing me, heading down the stairs to the pool.

I don't have a choice.

I move up behind her, keeping low, and in the blink of an eye, just before she puts her foot on the first step, I come up behind her and clap a hand around her mouth. I don't put the knife to her throat, though, even though the instinct is there.

Immediately, she yelps and starts to struggle, until I growl into her ear.

"Is he here?"

She freezes, then relaxes when she realizes who I am, but only slightly. I see her hand ball into a fist.

"Mm-mm," she says, shaking her head no, and I don't sense a lie. Immediately, I release her, and she staggers back to clutch the balcony railing, glaring at my cool smile.

"Good," I say, tossing the knife up and catching it again as my shoulders relax. "That would make this reunion a lot more awkward."

"You?" I spit in total surprise and just a twinge of annoyed disdain. "You. Of *course* you're here. But *why* are you here? And don't you dare touch me like that again."

Dominick raises an eyebrow as he stares at me, still toying absently with the knife in his hands. If he was anyone else, I would be worried about him cutting his hands or slicing off a thumb or whatever. But I know without even having to ask that Dom is the kind of guy who can absolutely play around with a knife and not injure himself. Even right now, in this tense, risky moment, all my mind can think about is whether he would be just as deft with that knife in bed.

Come on, Hadley. Get it together, I scold myself.

"I know why I'm here, but I don't know why

you're here," he replies coolly. "So it would appear we both have questions."

"I don't have to answer to you. You lost those rights the other morning," I hiss icily, folding my arms over my chest as I balance back against the balcony. I gaze unblinkingly at Dominick, not willing to cede him even an inch. He may have the size and weapon advantage over me, and I know damn well that if he decides he wants to take me out, he can do so easily. Very easily. Effortlessly. With relish. I have no doubt in my mind that Dom has done much worse for much little provocation.

"No, that's right. You don't answer to me, but you're not a free agent, either," he says pointedly. "You have someone you *do* answer to."

"No. I work for myself. I follow my own passions. Nobody owns me," I retort, defiantly raising my chin and squinting at him venomously.

To my horror, Dominick does the one thing that I absolutely cannot abide.

He looks at me with something akin to pity on his handsome face. I can feel my whole body tensing up, my heart fluttering. Rage bubbles up inside my chest and it's all I can do to keep from shaking a fist in his face or cursing him out. I don't take pity. Not from anyone. And especially not from a guy who played me like a one-night-stand.

"Don't look at me that way," I protest. "You don't know a damn thing about me, Dominick. You don't know my life. You don't know who I associate with. You don't know me. Now, get out of here so we can keep it that way."

Dominick sighs exasperatedly, shaking his head. "You know I can't leave here, Hadley," he says, lowering his voice to that raspy, gravelly growl that sets my blood on fire. I feel my body stirring. Coming to life at the mere sound of his voice in my ears. I know if I just took a few steps closer, I would feel the power, the heat radiating off of his incredible body. I could smell his masculine scent, that musky pine smell that intoxicates me faster than a tequila shot.

"Why not?" I ask, annoyed at how petulant my voice sounds. Like a stubborn little girl. What is it about this man that makes me wilt like this? He makes me feel vulnerable in ways I never even thought possible. I hate that he has so much hold over me. It's not fair.

"I'm not holding this knife for a whittling competition," Dom replies slyly.

"What's your point, huh? Why are you here? This is... this is private property," I reply, unable to think of any other way to retaliate.

"Oh, and you're the owner, are you? Hadley, it sure looks like we're both trespassing here to me. Only one of us has a knife, and the other has nothing," he points out. "Now, it's time to talk. You need to tell me where Carl Owens is. If he's not home, then where the hell did he go?"

"Right, like I'd have any idea where that man goes when he disappears," I shoot back bitterly. "It's not like he gives me regular check-ins or anything. Carl Owens does whatever the hell he wants to do and he doesn't tell a soul about it. Not even me."

"Does that hurt?" Dom asks quietly.

I frown at him as though he's lost his entire damn mind.

"What? Does what hurt?" I snort.

"Does it hurt that he watches you like a wolf stalking a doe through the woods? That you have to answer to his every beck and call? Tell me, Hadley: when your boss tells you to jump, do you ask him how high?" Dominick says.

My mouth falls open as I gape at him. "You fucking jerk. Don't you talk to me that way."

"So, do you let Carl talk to you like that?" he pushes me further.

"This conversation is over. I don't have to stand here and let you insult me to my face. I have—I have other things to do. Places to go. You and your knife can do whatever you want, you psycho. I'm leaving," I insist. I turn on my heel to try and head down the stairs, thinking I'll just take the back exit through the gate on the other side of the pool. But before I can take a full step, Dominick grabs my hand and pulls me back, making me twirl slightly as I face him, our bodies only mere inches apart. The knife hangs at his side, thank god, but I can still feel every thump of my frantic heart in my throat.

"I can't let you leave like this, Hadley," he murmurs solemnly. "Your boss is a bad man. I know you have to know that by now. Owens fucked up. There comes a point when you lose so much money there's no hope of winning it back. And even though he's got you and the other girls running around frantic to earn him money, he's not paying his own dues. I'm sure you understand how that doesn't fly."

"With the mafia," I fill in, looking up at him wide-eyed. "Is that why he's gone AWOL?"

Dominick nods slowly. "Yes. He owes money. A lot of money. And the interest he owes can't be paid in cash, no matter how much you win for him."

"So he's supposed to pay with... what? Blood?" I murmur breathlessly, the whole picture starting to come together in my head as Dom stares down at me, those brown eyes ablaze.

"Your boss is a bad man," he reiterates, "but mine is worse."

"And Carl owes your boss money. A lot of it," I say.

"Yes. Too much. That's why I'm here," he replies.

"To kill him," I whisper. "Holy shit."

"Exactly," says Dom smoothly, without an ounce of affectation.

"I can't let you do that," I tell him, furrowing my brow. "He's a dick, for sure, and the way he treats us is criminal. But murder? You really think that's what he deserves?"

"What do *you* think he deserves?" he asks, quirking one thick, dark eyebrow.

"I don't know. But he probably deserves to go to jail, not just to be stabbed to death by a stranger in his own home," I tell him, although the longer I try to go on defending my boss, the less I want to. He's never done a damn thing for me that wasn't actually for him. He runs us hard. He treats us like chattel. For all intents and purposes, I should hate the guy. I guess I do.

"Come on, Hadley, it's not that difficult," Dom insists. "The rules are fast and hard in your world, and even more so in mine. Owens knew the risk when he started toying with the mafia. We don't accept late payments."

"So, you're mafia, too? I guess you are as much of a loser as the girls said you were," I retort seethingly. He doesn't seem offended, more like just slightly amused.

"You told your friends about me?" he asks, a hint of a smile tugging at the corners of his lips. "I apologize for not making a better first impression."

"You fucked the life out of me and took off in the morning," I state matter-of-factly.

"Well, duty called. Not that it's an excuse, but it's an explanation. Sorry for demanding my shirt back so rudely. It looked a hell of a lot better on you, but I couldn't exactly report to my boss without a shirt on. That would be a more interesting world if I could, but no such luck," Dom quipped, taking a step back from me.

I chew my lip thoughtfully, my thoughts spinning out in wild circles.

"What are you thinking right now?" he asks, peering at me warily.

"I'm thinking that if you want to ever see me again and make up for the way you took off the other morning, you're going to have to come clean. And I mean, about everything. No more secrets. No more hopping out of the shadows holding a knife," I tell him, putting my hands on my hips.

He smirks. "Sweetheart, I've already told you everything. It's a simple story. I work security at the casino, but the casino is run by the mafia. I'm an enforcer. When they need a rule or a deal enforced, I am the one they call on to get it done."

"So, sleeping with me was just a ploy to get closer to my boss?" I suggest.

Dom looks disgusted by the idea. "No. God, no. You and your colleagues are not my target. You're the pawns. I need the king."

"I don't take well to being called a pawn," I mutter, glaring.

A broad, mischievous smile spreads slowly across his face. "Well, would you rather be a queen?" Dominick insinuates, looking me up and down.

I feel an unbelievable wave of tingly warmth pass over my body. But I have to hold my ground. I can't let my feelings for him get in the way. This man is here to *murder* my boss. *Come on, Hadley, get it together!*

"Queen to a killer? Well, I have to say it's not the fairytale ending I used to dream about as a little girl," I said sarcastically. "Why can't you just... scare him? Get him to leave Vegas, keep out of your boss' hair."

"Hadley, if I don't do this, they'll just send someone else after him. Someone worse. Someone much more sadistic than I am. I'm here for a paycheck, but there are those who would do my job just for the thrill of getting blood on their hands. Is that what you want?" he tells me.

"There's got to be some other solution," I protest, shaking my head so that my fiery red hair bounces over my shoulders. "Besides, if you kill him, how can I know you won't come after me and my girls next? We're associates of Carl. Is the mafia picking us off one by one?"

"No. You're not involved. You're small fry," he says, then winces a little. "I don't mean it to be offensive. I just mean that you're not on their radar. Not yet. But if you continue to stand here and prevent me from carrying out my orders... that could change. I tell you that as a warning, Hadley. Don't let your boss's fuckup get you dirtied up, too."

"Dom, this is fucked up. You're not a *killer*. You

can't just... just... take someone's life like it's nothing, like it's just something you have to do at your boring nine-to-five."

"What else would I do? Just scare him out of town? Lie to my boss?" Dominick says.

"Yes. Exactly. All of that," I reply hastily.

"You're making this very difficult for me, you know that?" he says to me in a way that tells me he might actually be considering my words.

Dom is about to say something else when suddenly, my cell phone rings again. I hold up a finger to shush him and answer the phone, noticing with a chill down my spine that it's a number I don't recognize.

"Hello?" I answer softly, desperately.

"Hadley! I did what you said! I got away! I'm in a gas station, in the desert!" She sounds frantic, her breaths coming through the receive roughly.

"You escaped? How? Wait, no, that doesn't matter. Where are you? I'll come get you. Just hang in there, okay?" I tell her quickly, watching the look on Dom's face change out of the corner of my eye.

"What? This payphone keeps beeping at me! I can't hear you, Hadley!"

"Hold on, hon, just stay on the line," I command her, but it's like I jinx it, because a moment later the line cuts out again. And goes dead. I look at Dom in desperation, shaking my head as the words fail to come out of my mouth. I'm split. I'm being torn in two different directions. If I stay here, I can possibly prevent Dom from killing my boss, but I'll lose my chance to save Vanessa. But if I leave to try and track down Vanessa… Dom might go against his word and kill Carl.

What the hell am I supposed to do?

Can I trust Dominick not to kill him if I leave?

"Is that your friend from the other night?" Dominick asks warily.

I can tell he's trying not to show how interested he is. How involved. He frames the question like casual curiosity but I know it's more than that. His life, his job, his people—all of that connects with my life, my job, my people. He's trying to piece it all together, but I don't know yet if I can trust him if he does untangle it all the way. Whatever is happening to Vanessa is not his business. Yet.

"No," I lie quickly. "It's, uh, someone you don't know."

He narrows his eyes at me with suspicion, still toying with the knife in a way that I can't quite decipher as playful or threatening. He shakes his head.

"You're in over your head, sweetheart. This world you and your friends are falling into is not a habitable environment for women like you," he says rather cryptically.

I raise an eyebrow and wrinkle my nose. "Sorry, what was that? *Women like me?* What does that mean? What are you implying?" I retort. I don't stand for being condescended to or given an insult couched in advice.

"Well, are you or are you not a woman working under the thumb of a sleazy predator like Owens?" Dominick pointed out with a shrug. "Being involved with that kind of guy is never going to lead anywhere good."

"He's not my boyfriend. He's not my pimp. He's just my boss," I protest defiantly, even though my bravado is starting to slip. I know Dom is right. I would never have gotten roped into this big mess if I wasn't a recruit of Carl Owens. And even though I always try to convince myself that being a good enough gambler and making money for him through that channel would be enough to protect me from… the other ways in which he would contract me out for money.

If I make myself priceless, if I make him need me out on the casino floor winning games and matches and bringing home sacks of chips, then he won't make me do anything worse. I've heard the stories. I know what kind of man Carl is behind his faux-father-figure demeanor and his talk of teamwork. It's dawning on me that I could never be more valuable at a poker game than in some stranger's bed. My heart sinks as I think about Vanessa, who is probably meeting that same exact fate I'm dreading.

When it comes down to it, we may be brilliant, put-together, professional, strong women—but a predator like Owens will always just see us as chattel. Just assets to be auctioned off to the highest bidder. And to think there was ever a time I might have defended him…

"You know he deserves nothing less than death," Dominick says, his gravelly voice punching through the fog of anxiety clouding my head. I look up at him, a little taken aback. I blink a few times, feeling that muscle in my jaw tensing as it always does when I am trying my hardest to hold back tears.

Dominick is right. I know it. And maybe this makes me weak, but I still don't want him to kill Carl. There has to be another way. Right now, though, I don't have the time to stand here and stall the probably inevitable murder of my evil, conniving boss. I need to find Vanessa somehow. She said she escaped whoever captured her. I won't let them catch up and take her away again.

So I give Dominick one last long look, my eyes blazing with intention, with persuasion.

"Please, Dom," I begin quietly. "Don't do this. Don't kill him. I agree that he probably deserves it. I've seen his true colors, okay? I get it. I know who and what he is. Money is his god, and he will sacrifice everything and everyone to get more of it, and he doesn't care if it's abusive or awful. But there has to be a different way to handle this. I'm going to leave now, because someone I care deeply about is in trouble. That means I am trusting you, Dominick. I'm trusting you not to kill my boss."

Dominick regards me with a furrowed brow, a dark scowl on his angular face. I can positively feel the cogs turning in his head as he weighs my words, but I know I can't stick around long enough to see him make the decision.

"Will you let me leave here if I promise not to turn you in?" I ask him in a small voice.

He groans, tensing up and letting out a long, exasperated sigh. "Yes. I am trusting you, just as you're trusting me," he says emphatically.

"Thank you. Trust me, I won't say a single word," I assure him, making my way toward the stairs.

I watch him a little nervously as I disentangle from the conversation, but he doesn't make a move to stop me. I hurry down the marble steps to the backyard, bolt across the flawlessly-manicured lawn, jump over a flowerbed of zinnias, and open the side gate to let myself out. I make my way to the curb, then whip out my phone. I call a cab to come pick me up, every minute feeling like hours.

As the taxi rolls to a halt by the curb, I realize with a shudder of dismay that I don't actually know where to tell the driver to go. Vanessa wasn't able to give me coordinates or an address or anything. I hesitantly climb into the back seat, fully preparing to sound like a complete crazy person. The driver glances at me in the overhead mirror, looking bored out of his mind as he loudly smacks on chewing gum.

"Where to, miss?" he asks.

"Uh," I murmur, staring down at my phone, willing it to ring. I look up to meet the driver's gaze. I wrack my brain for a moment, piecing together the few mildly useful words Vanessa could give me. Station. The desert. Nowhere.

A gas station out in the desert, the middle of nowhere. Nevada has lots of those. But this one won't be too far from the city, I'd guess.

"Miss, do you have an address for me? We're wasting time," the driver urges me.

"Oh, I apologize. I don't actually have an address, but do you happen to know of a gas station out in the desert where... uh, where bad people go to do bad things?" I ask, wincing at how ridiculous my request must sound.

The look in my driver's eyes shifts and he slowly nods with understanding. "It's not where they do business, but there's a gas station I know of that the night folks like to use," he says, pulling the cab away from the curb. "Figure it's that place, if you're looking for bad people. Didn't figure you the type."

"Is it in this area code?" I ask him, showing him

the call history, and he nods.

"Yea, that's the one."

"And there's a payphone there?"

"Sure, though I don't know if it's in service anymore. Why do you want to go out there?"

"I don't want to talk about it," I tell him, leaning back against the seat with a sigh. It might be a dead end, but it's the only clue I have.

I stare out the window as the cab rolls along down the road, leaving the relatively quiet, remote neighborhood where Carl made his home. I turn back and watch my boss's swanky hideaway get smaller and less impressive as we drive away, until finally it disappears over the horizon. I turn back around, biting my lip and fidgeting with the cell phone in my hands. I can't seem to stop checking it nervously, making sure that the sound is on over and over again. It's just that I can't risk missing a phone call from Vanessa.

She says she's escaped whoever nabbed her, but who knows how close behind her captors might be. What if she didn't get very far? What if those assholes are still nearby, just sniffing her out? My stomach twists and turns at the thought that I might arrive there too late. Or, even more likely, I end up at the wrong desert gas station altogether, miles and miles of dusty red dirt away from where my closest friend and colleague is desperately waiting for a rescue.

That's a sobering thought. And following on its heels comes another dark thought, this one in a different direction but just as pressing. The clear picture in my mind that just won't fade away no matter how hard I try to shake it off: Dominick and his handy, glistening, sharp knife. I know whose body that knife is itching to carve up. And I can't deny that it would probably make the world a safer, better place for him to be gone.

Can I trust Dominick to leave Carl alive?

And perhaps more importantly, do I really want him to?

I can't help but think about Dominick and how strangely we have fallen into each other's lives. When I first met him, I assumed he was just like all the other guys who sidle up next to me at the casino bar, spouting off some smooth line and offering to buy me drinks to lower my inhibitions. I can see that kind of man coming from a mile away. Like a pointed shark fin cutting through crystal-blue waters, I know what sort of beast to expect. I know how they attack. And by now, I have long since learned how to defend myself. But Dominick disarmed me so easily. I tried to put up the usual walls, the usual deterrents. My sarcastic wit, my sharp tongue, my aloof demeanor. Everything from my blood-red stilettos to my well-practiced glare is meant to keep them from getting too close.

I'm not supposed to let them in.

I'm not supposed to let my guard down.

But he found a way. I feel helpless to resist him. It frightens me to think that if he were to magically appear next to me right now, he would make my heart pound and my body warm up. I can't pretend like my body isn't drawn to his like a moth to flame. I know he'll burn me if I get too close. Especially now that I know just how dangerous a life he leads. I thought *I* was living life on the edge, but I've never been ordered to kill a man.

The scenery as I stare out the window shifts from glossy high-rise buildings to smaller, humbler neighborhoods on the outskirts of town, to the wide red-gold expanse of the dusty desert. Cacti and strange, clay-colored outcroppings dot the landscape. There's something about this part of the world that fills me with a powerful sense of loneliness and awe. It feels like no man's land. It feels empty and yet full of mystery at the same time. And somewhere out here, at some podunk, middle-of-nowhere fill-up station, I hope to find my friend. I check my phone obsessively as we move farther away from Carl's hideaway, but I don't get any calls. My stomach aches, my heart racing as I search the horizon for signs of life.

Finally, I manage to just barely make out the shimmering form of a building in the near distance. I lean forward excitedly and point out the front windshield.

"Is that it?"

"Yes, ma'am," he says flatly. "That where you want to be dropped off?"

"Yes. But don't leave. I'm just here to… to collect someone," I say vaguely as I give him a folded fifty, "This is just a tip."

The cab rumbles down the road and pulls to a stop in front of the gas station. It's an ancient-looking place, the metal sign being devoured by crumbling rust. There looks to have been a time when there were multiple gas pumps available, but now it's just the one lonely diesel pump sitting in the middle, a puddle of colorful dark oil gathered next to it. If not for the dejected OPEN sign hanging at a jaunty angle at the front entrance, I would assume the whole place is shut down. The driver gives me a doubtful look.

"You sure you want to get out here?" he asks warily.

"No," I answer honestly, "but I have to. Wait for me," I order him as I step out of the vehicle.

"Sure," he says, shaking his head.

I don't know what exactly to expect here, or whether my hunch that this is where Vanessa is hiding is correct. I slip out of the cab, take a deep breath, and saunter up to the gas station, trying to exude placid calmness. I don't see her anywhere outside, so I push open the doors, which sets off a little dinging bell. The ancient-looking man behind the counter looks up at me with his wiry, bushy white eyebrows and seems surprised. I start making my way down the chips and cookie aisle, surreptitiously looking around. I don't see anyone here, much less someone who looks like Vanessa. My heart starts to sink. Maybe this is the wrong place, after all.

"Please don't tell me you're just here to use the bathroom," he says suddenly.

I whip around and give him a frown of confusion. "I'm not, but why?" I ask, folding my arms over my chest. The gas station attendant heaves a sigh and rolls his eyes.

"There's a young lady in there who's been hogging the toilet for going on an hour now. I've had to turn away two paying customers because she refuses to come out of there. My guess is she's hungover or something. You crazy kids are always taking it too far on your little club nights in the city," he preaches grumpily.

"The girl who's in the bathroom right now—what does she look like?"

The guy shrugs. "I don't know. Kind of like you. Real pretty. She's got dark hair, though, not pretty red like yours. About your age, I'd guess," he says.

I turn and bolt to the women's restroom at the back of the gas station building and start knocking on the door desperately. "Vanessa? Vanessa! Are you in there?"

"H-Hadley?" comes a tiny, meek, tearful voice from the other side of the door.

I can't help but smile with relief. "Yeah, it's me, hon. Open up."

After a moment of hesitation, I hear the door unlock and it starts to slowly open, Vanessa's tear-streaked and terrified face appearing in front of me. Her eyes dart around with fear for a moment and then her arm shoots out to grab me by the shoulder and yank me into the bathroom with her.

I try to protest, "Vanessa, what are you—" but she manages to pull me and lock the door so quickly I don't even have a chance to respond. I stare at her, looking her up and down in horror. Her dress is dirty, her knees scraped up and bruised. Her hair, usually so sleek and shiny, hangs limp and greasy around her petrified face. There are bags under her almond-shaped eyes and mascara-black lines track down her cheeks. Even her trade-mark dark red lipstick is smudged around her mouth messily.

She looks terrible.

I immediately grab some paper towels from the dispenser and dampen them with warm water, then take a few tentative steps toward my friend. At first, she instinctively steps back and shields herself with a little whimper, but when she remembers that it's just me, she lets me dab at her face. As I clean her up, I ask questions.

"Nessa, can you tell me how you got here?" I ask softly.

She's staring right at the floor, utterly downtrodden. "I was kidnapped as I was leaving the casino. I was trying to hail a cab in the dark. And then someone was grabbing me. It all went dark. Chloroform, maybe. When I came to, I was in a dark room. I heard… I heard something Carl said about wanting to clear his debts to the mafia? He told them, the other guys, that he had something more valuable than casino chips. He offered me up as part of the deal. But they got angry at him. I could hear them arguing. One of them said it was an unfair offer, that I'm not even worth half his debt," she sighs.

"Well, that's both disgusting and offensive," I retort fiercely.

"I know," Vanessa agrees, nodding. "But Hadley, that's not the end of it. There's more. When they asked for a fairer deal, Carl said he'd double his offer by… by throwing you into the mix, too. He said your name, Hadley. He wants to sell us both."

My heart is pounding.

Instinctively, I try to tell myself she misunderstood. That there's no way that Carl is going to sell us to the mafia, not for any reason. But there's a pit in my stomach, because I know that Dom was right. "How did you get away, Vanessa?"

"At one point they, uh, chloroformed me again. I woke up in the back trunk of a car. I was really scared and my whole body hurt. I could feel the car going really fast, so I knew there was nothing I could do. But then I felt it stop. Here. At the gas station. I heard the guy get out to pump the gas, and then he walked away. I heard his footsteps get softer. I was so scared, but I remembered something Monique taught me once when we were watching some police show together.

I kicked out the taillight and reached through it to press that button to pop the trunk. As soon as it was open, I closed the trunk and ran. I hid behind that huge saguaro not far from the gas station and I watched the guy get back in the car and drive off. I don't think he knew I was gone. And when he drove away, I just called you from the payphone and ran into the station and locked myself in the bathroom. I wanted to call the cops but... I was afraid. Besides, they wouldn't believe me. I know they wouldn't," she begins to cry, her shoulders shaking with emotion.

I put my arms around her, patting her on the back as she sobs into my shoulder. This is all worse than I even thought. Dominick was right on the money. I always knew Carl was a sleazebag who couldn't be trusted, but this? This is insanity. Selling us to the mafia like a couple of cows? Hell no. I won't stand for it.

"Vanessa, listen to me: the mafia doesn't forget a bargain. They'll be coming after us, and between the mafia and Carl, one of the two is bound to catch up if we don't split soon. So here's what you're going to do for me. I'm going to give you some money, and I'm going to get that nice cab driver out there to call up one of his colleagues to come get me. That nice man is going to take you to Reno. There, you're going to get on a bus. Make sure you buy a ticket to get as far from Vegas as you can go. Then find another bus station, another company, and take another bus even further. When you get there, you lie low, okay? Use the money I give you. Pay for a hotel. Not a crappy one, either. You put yourself up in a safe hotel and make it your basecamp. From there, you find a job. Something quiet. Be a bartender or a nanny or something. Get paid in cash and pay for everything in cash. Keep a stash of burner phones. Use one for a week and toss it. On to the next one. They'll forget us eventually, but for now, you're going to need to be paranoid to keep yourself safe," I tell her firmly, pushing back to gaze into her teary eyes.

She sniffles and nods. "But what about you, Hadley? Why don't you just come with me? They'll be after you, too. Just come with me. We can hide out together," she suggests.

I bite my lip. It's a tempting offer. Just leave all this mess behind and start over. But if I do, I'll be abandoning my money. My dreams of owning a home. Of traveling the world. Of broadening my horizons.

And I'll be leaving Dominick behind, too. Why does the thought of that bug me so much?

"I can't go with you," I tell her with a sigh. "I can't. One of us can disappear, but us together... It's too dangerous, honey. We need to split up. It'll be harder for them to trace us that way. Here. Take this."

I pull out my slick little patent leather wallet and yank out a stack of hundred-dollar bills. A thick stack. Vanessa's eyes widen as I force the stack into her hands. "Go out there and get in that taxi. Tell him to take you to Reno. Follow my instructions from there. You can do this," I assure her.

She looks heartbroken at first, and I know it's killing her to leave me behind. But finally, she nods and tucks the money into her pocket. "Okay. I'll try. Thank you," Vanessa says softly.

"Don't mention it. We've got to look out for each other in this world. Because you sure as hell know nobody else is going to," I tell her with a dry smile. "Go. Go ahead."

She looks like she wants to say something else, but she thinks better of it. Instead, she just hugs me tight for a few seconds, then bolts out of the bathroom. She leaves me to stand there, looking at my own reflection in the filthy mirror. What the hell am I going to do? Will I run away? Spend my whole life trying to outpace the mafia, always looking over my shoulder?

DOMINICK

The sound of my brass knuckles landing a solid blow on Carl Owen's right cheek-bone makes a satisfying crack as the bastard's head flies back, nearly knocking him over. Thanks to the soft white glow of the security camera screens, I can see the trickle of blood running down his face and staining his shirt collar as he trembles.

"Hey hey, none of that," I growl, patting his face and making him look up at me again. "You fall asleep on me and I'll make you regret it when you wake up."

"Please, I-" he stammers, but I interrupt him with another punch to the jaw that knocks a tooth out, sending it clattering across the floor.

I have Carl in one of the money counting rooms under the casino, surrounded by security camera live feeds while I deal with him. All things considered, he has it better than a lot of people I've interrogated. His clothes are still on, his joints are all intact, and I haven't yet been ordered to cut anything off him.

But I'm still trying to figure out why Jerry had such a sudden change of heart.

Not long after Hadley and I parted ways and I kept searching the house for any clues as to where Carl might have been, I got a call from Jerry himself. He told me there had been a change of plans regarding Carl.

That part isn't too unusual in the mafia. Deals change and get made in the blink of an eye, especially when the person in question catches wind that his life is in danger. People will give up just about anything to spare their lives from the kind of punishment the mafia can dole out.

But Jerry was pretty confident that I wasn't supposed to take *any* deal from Carl Owens. He was worth more than just the debt; he was going to be the message that makes sure the casino runs very smoothly for the foreseeable future.

Jerry didn't give me specifics, but he did call me back to the casino with a very interesting update.

The reason I couldn't find Carl at the house was that Carl was at the casino. Jerry told me he'd had a chat with Carl, and that he would soon be trying to leave the casino and head back to me. He wanted to keep Carl a little closer to home, so he had me intercept the guy in the parking lot.

I had to admit, waiting for him by his own car and watching his face go pale was a satisfying experience, after everything I'd heard about the scumbag. It was even more satisfying to tackle him to the ground and subdue him before having him dragged down here to the money counting room. As if it weren't obvious, this room doubles as an interrogation room of sorts. Can't see bloodstains in the carpet when the lights are off so often.

Simply put, Jerry gave me orders to beat the living shit out of Carl. He said specifically not to kill him, and with every punch, I'm curious to know why.

"Still with me, Carl?" I ask mildly as I flex my fingers, waiting for him to lift his head again. I reach down and take hold of his chin and force him to look up at my hardened face. "Can't tell you how bad it'll get for you if you pass out on me. Just telling you for your own sake."

"This shouldn't be happening, this is a mistake!" he blubbers. "I'm protected!"

"Is that so?" I chuckle, letting his head fall and pacing around him slowly. "Carl, I've got to hand it to you, you had a smart business model. But seriously, where'd you get the stones to try to pay us off with our own money? How stupid do you think we are?"

He struggles for words, and I slap him across the face before pulling a chair up and sitting across from him, putting the back in front of me and leaning my arms on it to stare at him.

"And how the fuck do you think you can treat your girls like that, huh?" I say in a lower tone. I shouldn't be talking about this part, but this one's personal. The idea of some fuck like Carl screwing over people like Hadley and Vanessa pisses me off on a deeper level than just business. "If Jerry starts thinking you're trying to flex nuts with us, don't think for a *second* that he'll hesitate to have me cut 'em off."

"Oh god, I'm so sorry," Carl sobs. "I-I just thought we had a deal! Y-you talked to Jerry, didn't you? He talked to you, right?"

There's that deal I was suspecting, but I don't know specifics yet. I start to wonder if I can use this to my advantage.

"Words are one thing," I say, standing up again and pacing slowly in front of him. "You proved that words aren't enough though, Carl. You've got nobody but you to blame for this."

"But- but I told them, I've got the girl ready to hand over to you!"

I pause.

Something clicks in my head, and my grip on my brass knuckles tightens. I know Hadley lied to me about it being Vanessa on the phone, and I know she was in trouble. Hadley believed I was going to kill her boss, and she wouldn't have left if what Vanessa said on the phone wasn't far more important than stopping me from murdering a man.

And now, this. I slowly make my way around behind Carl, and I reach down to take hold of his thin hair and pull his head back to look up at me.

"Oh, do you now? Maybe you're right, I don't think we're on the same page. Care to elaborate?"

"I-I-I made a deal with Jerry!" he says, suddenly energized by the thought that there might be hope for him. "I offered your people that simpering bitch Vanessa in exchange for clearing the debt, as-as-as an apology! B-but he said it wasn't enough!"

I let his hair go, and I slowly started to move across the room to a corner next to the security camera feeds.

"Go on," I say, sounding interested, as if I'm really second-guessing myself.

"So I... I told him," he breathed, sounding ragged and desperate. "I'd throw in another girl, the prettiest one out of the bunch! You've got to see her, she's stunning. Listen, you should be going to collect her right this second, give her right to Jerry! Or even better, just take her for a trial run! Her name is Hadley, she's staying at this very hotel! I've got her room number, you could go have a first go at her before your boss does!"

I find what I'm looking for, and a dark smile

crosses my face. I reach down and pick up an extension cord coiled up in the corner. I slip my brass knuckles off and put them in my pocket before picking up the three-pronged head of the extension cord, feeling the weight of the end of it.

Swinging that end around in a small, slow circle, I let Carl get a look at it as I approach him, glaring down at him with an uncaring expression.

"Two girls for a cleared debt, huh?" I say.

"Y-yeah, I swear! Check with Jerry, I'd bet my life on it!" he splutters, pupils widening at the sight of what I was approaching him with.

"I bet you would," I say coolly.

I lash the cord across his face, and the pointed metal catches him right on the sore cheekbone I'd been punishing a moment ago. He howls in pain as blood flies from him, and he barely has time to recover before I whip him again across the torso, and again, and again. I don't hold anything back. He deserves every one of the bleeding welts I'm giving him.

"I don't understand!" he sobs when I finally let up for a few moments.

"You don't need to," I say calmly. "You just need to let me know just how you're feeling." I swing the cord around again, seeing the glint of red on its tips.

I'm much, much more furious than I'm showing. It's tempting to kill Carl right now, orders be damned. Conscience be damned. Everything be fucking damned.

So, the fucker thought he could trade a couple of lives for his safety? Trade up the women he was using to make him rich? And Jerry just rolled with it? And to top it all off, one of the girls he's trading is Hadley?

I have all the info I need right now. I could beat Carl to death with this extension cord like I really, really want to, go grab Hadley, tell her to scatter the girls, then run off with her to wherever the fuck we want.

But then, I would just be hunted down by Jerry for the rest of his life. I'm good at lying low, but traveling with a partner would complicate things, especially since I'm sure Hadley would want to make sure Vanessa gets taken care of, too.

Decisions, decisions.

I lift the cord again, and Carl winces... just before I catch something out of the corner of my eye on one of the camera feeds.

A familiar figure is making her way into the casino, strutting with bold purpose. I'd know that stride anywhere, even if I can't see her face.

It's Hadley.

I clench my jaw. If she's here, that means she's in danger, because Jerry and his guys are going to be looking for her. Hell, I wouldn't be surprised if I get the order to grab her, but that would be all too convenient. I have to get out there to intercept her. If she doesn't know what she's walking into, it could be the end of the line for her. Even I might not be able to save her from whatever Jerry has in store.

Of course, knowing what I know about Hadley, she'd just as soon bite someone's dick off and get herself killed—still not a good outcome.

So, that leaves me with the question of what to do with Carl here.

I have to make a call fast. If Carl dies, then I'm going to have to move fast, because that will mean Jerry knows I'm his enemy. Either way, my working relationship with Jerry is about to end. But if he lives, it might buy me a little more time to figure things out with Hadley and maybe get a better plan of escape from this tight spot we find ourselves in. That, and I know Hadley doesn't want him to die. Whether she just has a conscience or doesn't want his blood on her hands, I don't know.

But damn, the satisfaction of icing this fucker right now would make it worth it.

He looks up at me with pathetic, evil, pleading eyes, and my grip on the extension cord tightens. I step forward and hoist my weapon once again, smirking down at the bastard.

"Smile for me, Carl. One more time."

"Hit me again," I murmur calmly, looking the blackjack dealer right in the eyes.

He looks at me with an expression of mild confusion and recognition, like he knows me from somewhere but can't quite place me. That makes perfect sense. He does know me. Or at least he knows *of* me. I've sat at his table before here in the casino, my body glowing under the glimmering lights, distracting my dealer and competition alike with the way my slinky black dresses show off my figure.

But tonight, I'm not dressed like that. All my designer gowns and cocktail frocks are neatly packed away into my suitcase. My stilettos, too. Even my makeup is toned down tonight, just a little mascara and a smudge of coral-pink tinted lip balm. I have pulled my hair back into a tight knot at the base of my skull, most of it covered with a slouchy beanie instead of wet-set into glamorous Hollywood waves. Instead of a fancy gown, I'm just wearing a pair of comfy jeans, accompanied by a plain, fitted white t-shirt and a pair of sneakers.

Tonight, I'm not playing my usual role. I'm not shooting for glamor and allure. I'm just a lowly, regular tourist off the street, playing the five-dollar games for kicks.

The dealer says, "Yes, ma'am," and hits me. The game starts over. I won the last round. I intend to keep winning, even though the victories are small. Inconsequential, even, compared to the millions I usually deal in. These fiver games are usually reserved for the amateurs, the first-timers, the bachelor parties who show up here with a couple hundred dollars to lose, who will inevitably be kicked out for being too rowdy before they get a chance to win back any of their losses. This is the table for people too poor or too scared to take big risks.

Usually, this is not my kind of table. I deal in the big bucks, and I never shy away from a big risk, either. It takes a lot to shake me, and a table full of senile retirees and sweaty college kids sure as hell doesn't even make a blip on my radar. I could wipe the floor with these players if I really wanted to. But in order to keep up my charade as just a regular tourist dropping in for a casual evening of Lincoln games, I have to lose every now and again. Besides, it might be good for my karmic scoreboard to let one of these goons win once in a while.

And I'm not here to make money, anyway. I'm not here to scam a bunch of losers or flirt with wealthy men or intimidate the competition. I'm here on a mission. I'm here to watch.

After rescuing Vanessa from that hellhole of a gas station bathroom and sending her on her way to freedom, I realized that I don't want to try and outrun my demons like that. Vanessa is different. She's a sweetheart, and she's brilliant at card-counting, but she's not like me. She's not as resilient. She aims to please. She just wants to live a soft, quiet, simple life in the safety of another city. Vanessa will have to change her name, take on a totally new identity. That's difficult to do, but I have no doubt that she'll be able to handle it. Especially with the massive financial boost I gave her to get started in her new life. All evening, as I sit here at the blackjack table, I have to remind and reassure myself that I did the right thing by sending Vanessa packing. What else could I have done for her? Clearly it isn't safe here in Vegas anymore. Carl won't protect us. He can't. And he's the one trying to use us as a human shield in the first place: our bodies, our spirits in exchange for his freedom. His debts, *mine* to repay.

But I'm not going down without a fight. That's why I've come back here. I may be in a sort of disguise, but that doesn't change the fact that I've essentially just walked right back into the viper's den. I used to be a predator in this environment, stalking through the casino looking for an easy win, a weak competitor to bring to his knees. Tonight, though, I come here as prey. I know this casino is crawling with mafia guys, enforcers who will do anything to stay on their boss's good side. And by now, I'm certain they must have discovered that Vanessa is missing. That's bound to piss off the mafia boss, losing one half of his debt repayment.

I'm the other half, hiding in plain sight. I'm doing my very own reconnaissance mission, even though it means I have to sneak around right under the mafia's collective nose. But if there's one thing my years in this industry has taught me, it's the value of knowing thy enemy. And my enemy just happens to be here in this casino somewhere, skulking through the shadows, brimming on the edge of a crowd, eyes peeled for the likes of Vanessa or me.

Even as I sit here playing the game as though I haven't got a care in the world, I'm actually on edge. I don't normally wear shades when I play poker or blackjack, as I consider my eyes part of the alluring package. They're just another asset with which to entrance and confuse my competitors. But this time, I've got my gigantic shades on to hide where I'm looking. Behind the oversized tinted lenses, my eyes dart around, gathering information, watching out for anyone suspicious.

It's nearly midnight now. I've had one hell of a long damn day, but I'm not even tired. All I feel is this electrical current radiating through my body, keeping me on edge, keeping my eye on the enemy, wherever he might be hiding. I know they're waiting for me. I'm sure Carl has told them all about me. Hell, that bastard probably gave them my damn measurements or something like I'm a prized farm animal at a county fair. I was smart to wear a disguise tonight. Carl will have told the guys how I normally dress. They're looking for a movie star, but tonight I'm just any other tourist from out of town.

Some people might say I'm crazy for ever coming back here in the first place. This casino is the most dangerous location on the planet for me right now, and yet, here the hell I am. I know how much is at risk if I stay here. I know what's on the line. What these assholes put Vanessa through was a crime. That poor girl will probably spend the rest of her life trying to recover from it. I can only hope that one day she'll land herself one truly phenomenal and non-judgmental therapist to help her work it all out.

As for me?

I would rather saunter right up to the beast and fight it with my own fists than run away. It's totally against my character. I considered taking off for a brief moment. Who in my position wouldn't at least give it some thought? But I realized that I would rather die fighting than spend the rest of my life looking back in fear.

Besides, there's another reason I couldn't get myself to leave town: Dominick.

I want to see him again. Are my priorities a little askew? Maybe. But then, I've never lived a normal life. I've never obeyed the rules before. So why now? I like Dominick. My body *loves* Dominick. And even if he's involved with the mafia, I know there's more to him than that. I could see it in his eyes when we were together. I could feel it in the way he touched me.

He could've turned me in to his bosses when he had the chance. I was literally right within his grasp at Carl's hideout house. And yet, he let me go free. That tells me something: that he's not as loyal to the mafia as they probably think he is. In turn, that means he might just prove useful to me. Instrumental in taking down the assholes who hurt my friend and who are scheming to hurt me, too. I am not a prized cow. I'm a damn woman, and I'm taking fate into my own perfectly manicured hands.

I win the game in front of me and the other players all groan with annoyance. I give them a little smile and decide to take pity on them. I excuse myself from the table, collecting my meager winnings as I leave. I'm on my way to a low-level poker game when my eyes lock onto something that jolts me from my head to my toes.

A familiar pair of intense, brooding eyes meeting my gaze from across the room. It's Dominick, dressed to the nines, but clearly working security. I can't believe it took me this long to figure out. When I first met him, I assumed he was some wealthy, bored playboy by the way he was dressed. I see now that's part of his ruse. *Well played,* I think to myself as I give him a wry, meaningful smirk. We found each other. Perfect.

I casually head toward the bar, walking slowly and pretending to text on my phone as an excuse to keep my head down. But before I can reach the bar counter, a large hand lands on my arm. I follow up the swell of his forearm, his biceps, his shoulder, up to look him in the face. Again, I am struck by how startlingly good-looking he is. Cheekbones hewn from pure marble, a jawline so powerful I could imagine sitting on it like a throne fit for a princess. There's an urgency in his eyes. A burning fire.

I wonder if it's burning for me.

"What the hell are you doing here?" he hisses, leaning in close so that his hot breath tickles my ear. A delicious shiver runs down my spine, and I can feel his heat radiating off of his chiseled body so close to mine.

"Observing the enemy," I answer plainly in a whisper.

"Are you out of your mind? They're looking for

you, Hadley. You can't be here right now. It's too dangerous," Dom insists.

"Well, you're one of them," I remind him with an air of defiance. "Are you going to turn me over to your bosses? Are you here to take me, Dom?"

He stares at me hard, a conflict waging in his eyes. I see that muscle twitching in his jaw. He doesn't move. Doesn't answer me. I roll my eyes and scoff, turning to walk away. But he catches me again with his hand on my arm, only this time his fingers close around my delicate wrist and I look back at him with a flash of indignant fury.

"Let me go," I growl between gritted teeth. But at the very same second, I notice what looks like several drops of bright red blood staining the starchy white cuff of his sleeve. I look up at him with worry, my fierce mask slipping away for a moment as genuine concern for him seeps through. I can't help it. I don't want him hurt.

But he's still on the enemy side. For all I know, he got that stain from carrying out mafia business. And when I happen to see two thick, beady-eyed enforcer types look our way from across the crowded casino, my heart sinks down to my stomach. I know I have to get out of here.

Now.

"Shit," I whisper, my eyes going wide. "They've seen us. Thanks a lot, Dom. Now, let me go so I can make a run for it."

I try to jerk my arm away, but when Dominick looks back to see the same enforcers I saw, he turns back to me with a conspiratorial look on his face. "Yes. You're right. You need to get the hell out of here. But without my help, you won't even make it out of the building. Follow me," he insists, starting to pull at my arm.

I hold back for a moment, narrowing my eyes and sizing him up.

"Come on, Hadley," he growls, those gorgeous eyes full of worry.

I bite my lip, feeling like either option is a trap.

Can I trust him, even though he's behind enemy lines?

"Try to keep an even pace, but don't look like you're in a hurry," I instruct her as we walk down the hallway toward the elevator to the garage.

"Why aren't we running?" she asks in an equally low tone.

"Because those guys who were watching us might think I'm already delivering you to Jerry, if we're lucky," I say. "But that's only going to last as long as someone watching us through the cameras doesn't catch on."

"How long do you think that'll be?"

"Not long enough," I growl as we step into the elevator. Once we're inside, I hit the button to take us down to the garage, and just before the doors close behind us, I see the two other enforcers heading toward us. One of them raises his hand for me to hold the door.

When I don't, I know there's a very good chance our cover has just been blown.

"Right, so we might have guys headed down the stairs to cut us off," I say, taking a deep breath and rolling my shoulders back before glancing up at the camera in the elevator. "Thankfully, the elevators are quick, and I'm not parked far from the doors. As soon as they're open, we're going to start walking, and walking fast. We're headed for the black Aston Martin. Beeline."

"You were just looking for an excuse to tell me you drive an Aston Martin, weren't you?" she remarks casually. I crack a smile.

"Maybe a little."

The doors open the next second, and I slip out after taking her hand before they can even finish opening. I don't hear the sounds of shouts and gunfire, so I take advantage of that—pedal faster when you're rolling downhill, so to speak. My car is in sight, and I click it unlocked as I hurry around to the driver's side.

Seconds later, we're seated, buckled, and I'm pulling out of the garage in the smoothest car in the garage.

"No cars full of goons chasing after us with machine guns hanging out the passenger windows," she remarks as we pull out onto the Vegas streets. "Think they're really onto you?"

"They could be," I admit. "And that could mean they're just not telling me yet. No way to know. This is how things go in our line of business. I might not find out until months from now that Jerry knew anything, and I'll get gunned down when I finally let my guard down when I'm least expecting it."

"Sounds like a real fun time," she says.

"A hoot."

But sure enough, about fifteen minutes in traffic pass as I try to weave around and lose any possible pursuers, and I don't see a trace of anyone tailing us. I recognize most of the security staff and their cars, anyway, so I know what to look for.

Hadley is quiet at first, just staring out the window or glancing in the mirrors, watching for the same things I'm watching for.

"So, we're out of the dragon's den," she says at last. "For better or worse. Where exactly are you taking me? I don't think I've decided if you're my savior or my kidnapper yet." She's smirking, but I know it's only half a joke, given what she suspects about what I did to her boss. I still don't know why it bothers her so much, but I'm not just going to walk all over her wishes. That *would* make me her kidnapper.

And that's not me.

"I've got an apartment off the Strip that the mob

doesn't know about," I say, almost reluctant. *Nobody* knows about the apartment I'm taking her to. I don't even know why I'm taking her here, it would be just as easy to pay cash for a hotel room somewhere. But I need somewhere I'm absolutely positive is secure, and hotel security is easy enough to bribe for information.

I know that from experience.

But it's important that Hadley trusts me if we're going to keep moving together, whatever it is we're moving toward. I hope I don't come to regret that trust, but I'll never know if I don't try.

"Side-hideout, huh?" she says, arching an eyebrow at me and tilting her head to the side. She pauses for a moment as if thinking about what she's about to insinuate before saying, "Sounds like things aren't as secure in the mob as you let on."

I give her a narrow glance, but my face doesn't shift. Nothing gets past Hadley. She's got an eye for this kind of thing that even most of my fellow enforcers don't have.

"You've seen firsthand what things are like on the underbelly of Vegas," I say. "It shouldn't be a surprise, but yes, you're right. I'm ex-military, I know how quickly those of us not yet made can wind up thrown under the bus, if we aren't careful. I hedge my bets. It's the only way to survive in a game like this."

"Good to know I've been swept off my feet by

someone who plays it safe," she says with a teasing smile, perching her chin on her hand as she looks at me thoughtfully. "So, what's your plan now, besides dancing closer to the fire?"

"Now would be a good time to level with each other about everything we know so far," I say bluntly. "Because there are two assholes who've been playing us for chumps, and they're going to keep doing that until we can outsmart them."

"Alright then, since you're leading, why don't you tell me first?" she says. She's trying to weasel me into giving her the advantage, but she'll be disappointed if she thinks I have anything that'll give her the reason to run off that she wants so badly.

"How about this: question for question," I say, smirking over at her, and she seems to like that idea.

"Fine. Shoot."

"Did you find Vanessa?"

That question seems to legitimately surprise her, and it makes her uneasy at the same time. She opens and closes her mouth a few times, struggling to find a safe reply.

"Yes," she says at last, carefully. I wait for more, but she doesn't give any.

"So, it's gonna be like that, is it?" I say.

"My turn," she says. "Why do you want to know if I found Vanessa?"

"You're not very sportsmanlike at this game," I chuckle, but I need to give her a little slack if I want more in return. "I asked because she's in as much danger as you, and I want to make sure she's safe. My turn. Is she safe?"

"Yes," she says, seeming to relax just a touch. She thinks for another moment. "I made sure of that personally. She's not as frail as she made herself look. Okay, so, why are you helping me?"

"I like you more than my boss," I say. She seems a little taken aback by the simplicity of the statement, and I raise an eyebrow at her. "What? Money isn't everything, you of all people should understand that." Her face is still suspicious, but she seems amused by all this.

"So what, you just like the thrill of it?" she asks, and I hold up a finger with a smug smirk.

"Ah-ah-ah, question for question, remember? Do you know *why* I pulled you out of the casino?"

"Because your boss wants me," she says. "As well as Vanessa, which is why Vanessa had to go into hiding, and presumably why you're taking me into hiding. If you'd wanted to kill me or turn me over to your boss, you'd have done that already."

"You learn fast," I say, pleased.

"Learn fast or die young," she says without missing a beat. "Did you kill Carl Owens?"

My eyes flit to her again, briefly.

"You asked me not to."

"That doesn't count as an answer!" she says, furrowing her brow.

"We're here."

I cut us off by pulling into my space at the modest apartment building I keep as my safehouse. The garage is secure, and I keep a tarp over my car when I come and go, so the chances someone will come checking around for my ride are as low as I can get them. She looks uneasy, understandably. She still isn't sure if she can trust me. I get out of the car with her, pull the tarp over it, and make my way to the stairs to start climbing.

"I could run, you know," she says, more interested to see how I respond to that than actually threatening to try it.

"And then you'd have the same problem I'd have," I say mildly as I get to the door of my place, turning the key and glancing at her. "You'd have Jerry Laskin siccing his dogs on you for the rest of a very short, exciting life."

We step inside to what I like to think is a modest place. It doesn't have much personality to it, not enough for my liking at least, but it isn't a minimalist eyesore either. It has the basic amenities of any other southwestern home, and most importantly, a comfortable bed and large bathroom. Those are two things I've come to treasure over the years.

"Make yourself comfortable," I say, gesturing to everything in the house as she walks in and looks around curiously. I slip my suit jacket and toss it to the couch. "I keep canned food stocked, so it's not five-star dining, but-"

"You didn't answer my question," she interrupts me, approaching me at the entrance of the hallway that leads back to the bedroom. She has a look in her eyes that tells me she won't be distracted or put off any longer. She's resolute.

"Didn't I?" I say as I finish rolling my sleeves up to the forearm.

"Don't play dumb," she says, teasing tone gone from her voice. "I haven't played dumb with you, so don't you start with me. Did you kill him?"

I narrow my eyes, trying to read her, but she has a gaze like pure steel. Neither of our strong wills are able to budge, and I know there's not going to be any slipping around her attention.

"Why do you care for his life?" I ask softly, taking a step toward her.

"I don't," she says, holding her ground. "But I didn't get into this business for blood."

"You sound like me when I first started out."

She reaches up and grabs my tie, jaw set, glaring me in the eye.

"I'll ask you one last time, and if you don't give me a straight answer, I can't stay here in good conscience. Did you kill him?"

We glare long and hard at each other for what feels like an eternity.

"No," I finally say.

The tension between us lingers, and I can feel her grip on my tie not slacking as her eyes search me for lies. I can't get over how impossibly beautiful she is, especially when she's showing the real passion in that brilliant mind of hers.

Then, to my surprise, she pulls me towards her by my tie and kisses me on the lips.

Immediately, my body responds. I reach around her ass and pull her close to me, pinning her against the wall so she can feel the hardness she's been stirring up between my legs. She groans into the kiss, and I feel her tongue pushing into my mouth.

I let it in, and our tongues touch each other as I reach up with one hand and grope her breast. I want to drag her back to the bedroom, but I don't know if I can wait that long.

The energy between me and Hadley is intense and chaotic. She's a cunning mind, the likes of which I've never seen. Her body is on fire, and the moment we're together, we can't stop moving and grinding. We're so drawn to each other that even if I wanted to screw her over, even if all I cared about was money and all I wanted was to climb higher and higher in the ranks of the Vegas mafia...I don't think I'd be able to resist Hadley. She's far beyond anything I've ever experienced.

She reaches up and starts tugging my tie off, and I help her slip it over my head. But I leave it tied, and I grab her wrists, slipping them into it, then tugging the tie snug around her wrists. She looks up at me, bound, and the look in her eyes makes me unsure if she wants to fuck me or try to grab my knife from me.

I open the front of her pants and slip my fingers into her underwear while my other hand holds her bound wrists up above her head. My face looms over her, never breaking eye contact as she glares at me, full of anger and lust.

It feels like we both have words on the tips of our tongues, but we can't decide if it's a show of weakness to be the first one to speak. When neither of us can do so, we meet in a hot, fierce kiss again as my fingers find her wet folds. She's hot and slick, and I can't help but chuckle when I feel that.

"You," she says when we break the kiss, "have no room to make fun of me. I can feel how hard you are. You want this just as much as I do." She pushes her hips against mine to let my thick cock brush against her thigh, and it pulses, betraying me.

"Got me there," I growl, taking my fingers out and slipping them into my mouth to lick clean before I pull her pants down. "I'll have to show you just how hard I am."

She kicks her pants off the rest of the way, along with her shoes, while I work my pants open and let my cock spring free. She gasps as soon as I press its underside to her groin and start grinding against her.

My whole body awakens at her touch. Her lips are so wet and desperate for me to fill them, and right now, I don't want to hold anything back. We have too much tension, too much raw energy to work out on each other, and hardly any time to do it.

She jumps up and wraps her legs around my waist while I pin her against the wall, and I catch her ass, holding her up with ease as our foreheads touch. I'm still holding her hands tied above her head, and the blush in her face tells me she's enjoying what's happening to her.

I push her body up a little further and let the tip of my cock make contact with her pussy, and I listen to the almost musical sound of her gasp. I bring my face to hers, and as we kiss, I let her sink slowly onto me.

With every inch she slides down my shaft, I feel her whole body tense and her back arch as she sinks down onto me all the way to the hilt.

I start rocking back and forth, and within seconds, that turns into aggressive, energized rutting. I pin her tight against the wall, using one hand to remind her how much control I have over her arms while the other hand holds her up. Each time I buck into her, I feel my crown grind against every smooth inch of her inner depths, and my cock throbs inside her in desire. And each time, my arms work together in perfect sync to turn her body in such a way that she gets the most out of every thrust.

Her cheeks are flushed, and her breathing is quick and desperate. As my rhythm gets fiercer, I can see the tension and desire welling up in her face. She cracks her eyes open to look at me, and when she does, I can't help but let go of her wrists and bring my hand down to grab her hair. I tug her back gently to expose her neck while I fuck her.

She lets out an excited gasp as my teeth graze her, and I feel her getting tighter around me. She desperately wants to bring her arms down and wrap them around me, but I remind her how much control I have over her by pulling her hair the other way and ravishing the other side of her neck.

My hand grips her ass tighter, and I feel the tell-tale signs that she's close to the brink. I start letting myself go thrust by thrust, letting my pulsing cock free its inhibitions and start to release more and more tension and precum with each new piston.

Everything about her fills me with pure, raw desire. Her mind works faster than some of the finest criminals I've ever known to walk through my doors, and she's absolutely more dangerous than any of them. Her body feels like it was made to meld with mine, and the fact that she gets such satisfaction out of me is even better.

I get faster and faster, losing my precision, and something about that raw, bestial vigor I fuck her with sends her spilling over. She lets her jaw fall open as an almost worried moan escapes her lips, which I silence with a kiss as we start coming together.

My seed empties into her as we let out desperate groans together, never breaking pace, never stopping our motions, never letting up for a moment. My knees almost go weak as the force of the orgasm wracks my body, and she tries to squirm this way and that, but I keep her pinned, taking every last drop of me.

When it's finally over, I feel utterly spent inside her, and she looks at me with that flustered, glowing face that haunts my every spare thought anymore.

"Does that answer all your questions?" I growl.

"*Hadley, are you ready to go?*"

At first, it's difficult for me to distinguish where the question is coming from. It's like all the feeling in my body, all the strength, has been sapped. My lifeblood, the electrical currents that bounce through my limbs, carrying on a conversation with my brain, it all seems dampened. Softened. Muted, even. I want to turn my head and find the source of the voice calling out to me. The tone is so familiar. So urgent, but with an eerie singsong quality that puts me on edge.

Someone is calling my name. And slowly I realize that the voice isn't inside my head. It's out there somewhere in the blackness, reaching like a ghostly, pale arm from the shadows. Extending to me. Asking for me. Trying to pull me along.

"Come on. We don't have much time. Follow me," urges the voice. *It's a female voice, one I recognize. She's*

got a slight tremble to her words. I can vaguely summon up an image of her face on the projection screen of my mind. She's there. Her face, looming smooth and clear as a full moon, but with sad eyes and a downturned mouth.

She's worried for me. Deep down, I know how odd that is. Because normally, I would be the one worried about her. She's holding out a hand. I can feel the warmth radiating off of her body even though she's out of reach, out of sight. Like my eyes just won't focus. It's all refracted light, bowing and shining and folding in on itself. It takes all my willpower to figure out how to part my lips. My body is slow to carry out the demands of my brain. But it does. It works. Air swells in my vocal cords like the pumping of some great pipe and I manage a word.

"How?"

It's the most direct question I can cough out.

She hesitates. I feel her blinking at me. I think she's annoyed with me. I wasn't supposed to question it. I was supposed to do what she told me. It's not anger so much as exasperation, though.

"There isn't time. Hadley, are you coming or not?" she asks.

"I'm trying, Vanessa," I respond in a mumble. "It's hard to get away."

"That's only because somebody has you trapped," she admonishes me, shaking her head so that her glossy hair tosses from side to side. "He's got you caught here."

"He would never hurt me," I protest. My voice is barely a whisper.

"Maybe not on purpose," she says pointedly. *"But the longer you wait, the harder it will be to disentangle yourself. You sent me away. Do the same with yourself."*

"It's not so simple, Vanessa," I tell her, with a hint of pleading.

Vanessa tilts her head, light shining dimly where her facial features should be.

"You have to choose," she tells me, and finally her face begins to emerge from the fog of double vision and blurry shadow. Vanessa is wearing an expression of concern. She looks beautiful and healthy, but cold, even as I sense her heat. She's alive. But there's something missing. Maybe she isn't real.

Well, yeah, she's not real, *I think to myself with a burst of sudden clarity,* you're having a dream. None of this is real. And yet… you still have to answer her.

"Make sure you choose the right path. Both will be dangerous but one will walk you straight off a cliff," Vanessa chides me. She folds her arms over her chest, regarding me with more pity than fury. Somehow, that's worse, though. I can't abide pity.

"I can handle myself," I assert defiantly. She raises one perfectly-arched brow.

"Ego will get you nowhere," she says. *"Meet me when you get free."*

"Where are you going?" I ask, my heart sinking as Vanessa's shimmery figure slowly turns to walk away from me toward the engulfing darkness.

She doesn't reply. I try to step after her, but my body is locked again. I can't move. I can only stand here helplessly as Vanessa disappears. And when she's gone, I feel a powerful fear begin to surge through my body. Goosebumps raise up on my skin. There's a sensation of icy cold water dripping down my spine.

It's totally quiet now except for the quickening thump of my heart. And in between the beats is another rhythm. Soft, sure footsteps behind me. The tiny hairs on the back of my neck stand up. I'm not alone here anymore.

Scarcely able to breathe, I close my eyes and try to turn and face whoever or whatever is coming up behind me, but I can't. I can't move. I'm frozen here, listening helplessly as the approaching creature's breathing gets louder and closer. Almost ragged. Animalistic.

I feel a puff of hot breath on the back of my neck and suddenly all the feeling comes pouring back into my body. I let out a scream of terror and start thrashing around, confused and horrified, fearing for my life.

"Help!" I gasp, the pillowcase under my cheek sticky with saliva. The word is a soft, fervent whisper—just loud enough to wake myself up out of a dream.

I lie there with my eyes wide for a few moments, just letting my chest heave with painful heartbeats. There's a faint glow of sunlight peeking out around the rectangular edges of the blackout curtain hanging over the window. It's mostly dark in the bedroom, but those edges lend just enough light for me to look around and find my bearings. It all comes back to me. Slowly.

I am in an apartment. A secret apartment. One belonging to none other than the violent, dangerous man who was slated to kill my boss. I'm with him now. It's his breath I can feel ticklish and hot on the back of my neck. His hand resting on my hip as he breathes in and out calmly.

We slept together...again. What kind of a reckless fool am I turning into? What is it he has over me? What power is he using to keep me around even though I know perfectly well that he is nothing but trouble. I turn ever so slightly to look back at him over my bare shoulder. That impossibly handsome face looks stoic and thoughtful even in sleep. I wonder what he dreams about. Surely he has the same fucked-up, seemingly prophetic dreams that I have. Anyone who lives such a high-risk lifestyle must dream about dark things. Right?

Unless he's some kind of sociopath who doesn't feel the same way I do. Maybe all of this mess, the casinos, the hunt, the thrill, maybe it's all just nothing to him. Maybe he sleeps easy at night because he doesn't have the same lingering doubts and regrets I do. Sure, I know how to make myself cold. I know how to play the game. I can be aloof. But I still have feelings. I still have emotions that guide and trap me from time to time. I still have morals. Does Dominick feel that way, too? Is he still human? Or is he empty inside? Maybe he really is the monster from my dream.

But that's a lot to assume, especially of a man as unreadable and enigmatic as Dom.

He is still asleep, even though I'm awake. I'm pleased to see that my little outburst wasn't enough to disturb him. Right now, I need him to keep sleeping. I need him to be oblivious while I crawl out of bed and go looking around.

If there's one thing I have learned in all my years in my very niche industry, it's the value of a good reconnaissance mission. Know thy friends. And know thy enemy even better.

Inch by inch, using up every scrap of patience I can cobble together, I begin to slide out from underneath Dom's arm. His hand slips down my hip to the bed with a gentle thud and I wince, grimacing as I wait for the inevitable sounds of him waking up. But it doesn't happen. He's still asleep. Apparently, he's a much heavier sleeper than I would have guessed. I manage to scoot out from under the sheets, shivering as my bare skin meets the cool air.

I glance around, squinting in the low light for my clothes. Then I remember that we fucked out in the living room. My clothes are probably still there, wherever he tossed them in the heat of the moment. I blush to myself a little, surprised at how sheepish and bashful I feel about the whole thing. It's uncharacteristic for me to feel that way. After all, it's just sex, right? It's not a crime.

I tiptoe across the bedroom, thankful to see that the door is ajar so I don't have to risk waking Dom up with the creaky doorknob or something. I simply push the door a little more open and slip through, padding down the hallway stark naked, eyes sharp and on the hunt for clues of any kind. Something, anything, to tell me more about the real intentions and motivations of the man I just slept with. I find my panties and a clean, folded, oversized T-shirt draped over a chair. I put them on, just so that I don't have to be totally exposed while I snoop around Dominic's apartment. I walk into the kitchen and find the usual suspects: wine, whiskey, canned goods, the bare minimum level of cookery and utensils. I can tell he's not much of a chef. But a guy like him… he can afford to eat whatever he wants, wherever he wants.

There's a small television set hanging over the kitchen bar counter. I walk over and flick it on, hurriedly turning down the volume to low as I search for a news station. Finally, I find one and stand back to listen as a local news anchor gives an explanation. There's a glint in her eyes that tells me instantly, before she even speaks, that this is a juicy story.

Especially because she's standing out front of the casino I last worked in, and there are ribbons of glossy police tape behind her, cordoning off a crime scene. I bite my lip, feeling my stomach twist with anxiety.

"The unidentified body of a man has been discovered in an alleyway, just outside the walls of a well-known casino. The police have given no comments, and the victim's identity has not been released. We will do our best to keep the public notified every step of the way. You can count on me," the reporter declares firmly.

"Shit," I murmur, my hand flying forward to turn off the set. The screen goes black and I stand there staring at my dark reflection in the glass, my chest heaving visibly as my heart pounds. God. What is going on?

The body of a man. Outside the casino.

I'm no idiot. I can put two and two together. I just can't believe I was ever stupid enough to believe his cockamamie dodging of my questions. I just let him lie to me. I let Dominick twist and bend me around. I let him into my world. I don't do that for just anybody. I live a solitary life and it's supposed to stay that way, and yet, I let him in.

And now look what's happened. I knew it. I knew he killed Carl.

I can't believe I trusted him.

I bite the inside of my cheek to keep tears from burning in my eyes as I storm out of the kitchen. I walk into the living room and start rifling through

Dominic's stuff. I pull books off the shelves. I toss blankets and pillows on the floor. I move the couches to look under them on the floor. I roll up the fancy Persian rug. I check all the hidden spaces behind the television, inside the drawers, inside the vents. I don't even know what I'm looking for specifically. I'm just searching. Maybe for a reason. Maybe for something to tell me I'm wrong.

I move down the hallway to the guest bathroom and step inside, my hands shaking as I go through every item on the counter, in the shower, under the sink. And it's there, hiding behind a roll of toilet paper, wrapped up in more toilet paper, that I find the smoking gun in the form of a set of brass knuckles.

Brass knuckles covered in blood.

"Fuck," I murmur to myself, shaking my head as I kneel on the bathroom tile. There it sits, gleaming and slick with blood. Almost glowing, like some mystical force has guided me to find it. This is proof. Evidence that Dominick has not been as honest with me as he should have been. Proof that he's the bad guy. That he went against my wishes.

The body in the alley. The bloody knuckles.

"Damn it, Dominick," I hiss through gritted teeth. I've got to get out of here.

"What the hell are you doing?" comes a deep, annoyed voice from off to my right. I'm so startled that I gasp and fall backward onto my ass, my eyes widening as they fall on the tall, hulking figure in the doorway.

Dom.

I frantically scoot backwards until my back is pressed against the cold, white porcelain of the bathtub. I stare up at him with what I hope is defiance but which probably looks more like terror. And Dominick looks pissed. Betrayed, almost. He's standing over me in nothing but a pair of boxers that hug his thighs and do very little to disguise the massive cock between his legs. I gulp hard.

"Are you snooping?" he asks, glaring down at me.

I shrug. "No."

He sighs and pinches the bridge of his nose. "Don't lie to me, Hadley," he murmurs.

I scoff. "Me? Lie to you? Wow, that's rich."

"Come on. What are you talking about?" he asks.

"You know exactly what I'm talking about, Dominick! Jesus, I'm not an idiot. Yeah, it was stupid to ever believe you in the first place, but now—"

"But now, what? What, Hadley? What do you think your little Sherlock Holmes moment is telling you? What do you *think* you know?" he demands, somehow holding back even as his hands curl into fists.

"There was a dead body found in the alley outside of the casino. You're really going to try and tell me that has nothing to do with you? Seriously?" I snarl at him.

"You know, one of these days somebody is going to have to teach you how to mind your own business," Dominick snaps. "That would be a great lesson for you to learn."

"Don't you talk down to me like that," I snip, hastily getting to my feet. I'm realizing, though, how difficult it is to feel intimidating while dressed in only my panties and Dom's shirt. Still, I have to stand my ground.

"Wait, so you really think I have something to do with some body found in an alleyway? Really? Hadley, you know I'm not that sloppy. If I wanted to kill someone, I wouldn't leave his corpse out there in full view for the world to see. I may not be the innocent, law-abiding citizen you wish I was, but I'm a consummate professional. I keep my work clean," he says.

I raise an eyebrow and snort. "Yeah. Emphasis on 'consummate.'"

A flicker of something like a smile plays across his lips. "Don't tell me you have regrets about last night," Dom growls. "You enjoyed yourself."

"Maybe. But I shouldn't have. I should never have trusted a guy like you. I can't believe a single word that comes out of your mouth," I reply, trying to sound as icy as possible.

But he's stepping closer to me now. I can't be cold. Not when his heat is warming my body from head to toe. His closeness makes my breath hitch in my throat. He looks at me with hunger. With an almost predatory desire. I feel small in front of him. Dominick peers down at me, his chest bare, the muscles tensing.

"Do you want to fight or do you want to fuck?" he asks in a low voice.

My heart skips a beat. I can feel myself getting wet already, and I'm angry at myself for that. I hate that he has such a hold over me. It's like he alone carries the remote control that handles my body.

"I can't trust you," I whisper as he leans in close. His hand cups my cheek and I shiver.

"Why not?" Dom asks in a gravelly tone. "And why does it matter?"

"Surely you can understand why I'm a little tense here, Dom," I groan, rolling my eyes even as he traces my bottom lip with his thumb.

"Mhm," he mumbles. "Tell me."

"Well, there's a dead man outside the casino where I work. Vanessa was just literally kidnapped and I have no idea if I actually saved her life or sent her straight to the gallows. I'm up to my ears in some fucked-up mafia entanglement, and I just fucked the man who could be orchestrating the whole damn thing," I ramble, getting it all out in one rushed breath. "Oh, and my *boss* just sold me to the mafia for who knows what purpose."

Dom smiles wryly.

"Hmm. That does sound stressful. Let me take

your mind off of it. Let me show you that you can trust me, Hadley. Let me show you," he hisses as he leans in.

I hold my breath as his lips brush against mine, softly at first, then with more urgency. I can't help but moan as his tongue presses into my mouth. His hands slide down my face, one of them slipping down between my legs to stroke me through the dampening fabric of my panties while his other hand presses lightly at my throat. My eyes widen as he pulls back, playing with my clit and sending spirals of pleasure through my body. His fingers press around my throat, toying with my breaths. A spike of fear goes through me as I realize the power and control he has on me... but it just turns me on even more.

He reaches across the bathroom counter to grab what looks like a clean sweatband for working out. It's elastic with cloth over it, and when he starts to bind both of my wrists with it I inhale sharply, panting.

"Don't worry," he says gruffly. "I'll prove that you can trust me."

And with that, he scoops me up and carries me out of the bathroom. Hoisting me over his shoulder, he carries me down the hallway and into the bedroom, closing the door with his foot. He sets me down and walks me backward imperiously until my spine is against one of the bedposts. Without a word,

I let him lift my arms and bind my wrists to the post. I'm breathing hard, watching him slip off his boxers so that his enormous cock springs free, hard as diamond.

I am helpless, unable to make a move while his hands grope my breasts through the cotton t-shirt, toying with my nipples until I'm moaning and writhing against the bedpost. Dominick grabs hold of the t-shirt fabric and easily rips it open, making me gasp with surprise. He grins fiendishly and dives in to kiss and suck my nipples, his hands grabbing and fondling my breasts. I roll my hips, gasping and whimpering. One of his hands slides down under the waistband of my panties, tugging them down to bare my dripping cunny. He slips two fingers inside me, pumping hard while his other hand presses at the sides of my throat.

"Please. Fuck me," I murmur between gasps of pleasure.

"Do you trust me?" he asks darkly.

"I... I..."

At my hesitation, his hand tenses around my throat, the webbing pressing into me. It doesn't cut off my breath, or my voice. It's just... power. Completely controlled and contained power.

I swallow and his hand trails down over my collarbones, between my breasts, his touch forceful and moving with intent.

"I didn't hear you, Hadley," he chastises me, the

fingers inside my pussy pausing as his dark eyes catch mine. "I could do anything I want to you right now."

"Yes," I whimper, desire filling my throat.

"You want that?"

"So bad," I whimper, all the intense feelings of fear and desire mingling together to bring my erotic needs to a height I've never felt before. I'm practically trembling with lust, and already on the brink of orgasm. I grind against his fingers but he doesn't give in to my temptation.

"Do you trust me?"

I whimper, but I don't stop the truth from rolling over my lust filled tongue.

"Yes."

"That's what I wanted to hear," he growls, hastily pressing the engorged head of his shaft at my slick hole. I tense up as he shoves himself inside of me. I groan and close my eyes, letting my head fall back against the cold, hard bedpost as he fucks me, his hand still playing with my breaths at my throat.

Dominick doesn't go easy on me.

His hard cock slides in and out of my pussy fast and hard while he grips my throat, making me hold my breath for a few seconds, then loosening his grip to let me gasp. Every time, I get ever so slightly dizzy, and the pleasure ricocheting through my body is increased tenfold. I writhe and whimper and beg him for more, my words incoherent and stumbling into each other. All I know is that I've given up all control. Dom is the one in charge now. He is the one who decides what my body will feel.

And what I feel is beyond anything I've ever experienced before.

He pumps into me harder and harder, his fingertips toying with my breath until finally I'm hurtling toward climax. I gasp, feeling my face burn bright pink and my whole body tingle as he hoists my leg up over his hip, his cock spearing into me even deeper than before. At just that same moment, he gives my throat a quick squeeze.

And it's all over for me.

The most powerful, dizzying orgasm of my entire life shudders through me and I shake violently, going limp in Dominick's powerful arms. He cradles me easily, like I weigh nothing at all, while he fucks me through the waves of bliss. Just as I'm about to whimper for mercy, Dominick clutches me tight and I feel him come inside me, spurting hot seed deep within my slick pussy. We stand there pressed together and panting for a few moments, his hand sliding down from my throat. I gasp for a deep breath, but all I feel is exhilaration rather than fear. My eyes are locked with his as we breathe hard, trembling slightly as we come down together.

"Now, do you trust me?" Dominick asks softly.

I bite my lip, preparing to answer him. But just before I can say anything, I hear my phone go off on the nightstand. Dom and I look toward the phone, then back at each other. He hurriedly unbinds my sore wrists and I rush over on shaking legs to grab my phone.

"What is it?" Dominick demands.

I look over at him slowly. "It's a message… from my boss."

He stares at me hard, an expression of mild smugness on his face. I guess this means he didn't kill my boss after all. Jesus.

"You mean your boss you thought I killed?" Dominick points out.

I roll my eyes and sigh. "Yes. That boss. Can you let it go?"

"Sure. Sure. Yeah. But can you?" he asks sagely.

"I'm going to have to," I tell him, grimacing. "Because according to my boss, I have a game to play tonight."

DOMINICK

It's as frustrating to see Hadley losing as it is delicious to see her in that floor-length green dress that puts everyone else at the table to shame.

I'm curious as to what her game is. She came in tonight wearing that gown as if she was about to walk the red carpet, complete with elbow-length matching gloves and diamond earrings that make her look like a model in a museum. I *expected* her to come in and clean house yet again, especially when she sat down with this crowd. I recognize two of the men at the table as Silicon Valley millionaires, one of them as the heir to a cruise line fortune, and the fourth as an arms broker who has business ties in central Africa.

All of them are ripe for the plucking, but Hadley is getting trounced.

They're still playing for relatively low numbers— a few tens of thousands, which is pocket change to these people. But when I watch Hadley's flush get beaten by the heir's full house, I can't help but think that even I wouldn't have made some of the calls she's been making tonight.

I'm working again tonight, which means that at least for the time being, Jerry either hasn't caught on to me or is pretending he hasn't, for whatever reason. I'm still checking my car for explosives and looking over my shoulder every few minutes, but it would seem that I'm at least somewhat in the clear for now.

Mafia politics means things can change on a dime, without any warning, for almost any reason. It's a live fast die fast kind of lifestyle, and I don't plan on letting it swallow me alive anytime soon.

I keep an eye on the other guests as I make my rounds, but my attention is all on Hadley, and I never break my line of sight with her if I can. If my hunch is right, then the reason Jerry hasn't called out my odd behavior is because he suspects I'm keeping as much an eye on her as he is. He might think I've caught onto her and am just waiting for the right time for her to slip up.

Whatever gets me more time to watch Hadley work and make sure nobody's about to make a move on her, I'll take.

As she plays, I start to notice something unusual

about her. I've seen her play enough times now that I have a decent idea of what she's like when she plays. Normally, she's flirty and puts on a ditzy act to get the men's guard down, and she's still doing that today, but the guys are still winning. She's not off her game, though.

This is deliberate.

Every time she bluffs, I notice, she subtly tugs at one of her gloves, trying to straighten it out. It's a tell, and the experienced players at the table have picked up on it. But I know Hadley—she doesn't have any tells, or if she does, it sure as hell isn't that. She's making up a tell and using it to lull them into a false sense of security.

My suspicion gets confirmed before long. About an hour into her minor losses, I notice her give her tell once again. The Silicon Valley boys' eyes flit right to it, and they exchange a knowing look while Hadley pretends not to have notice. A matter of seconds later, the men at the table bet big, and the looks on their faces when Hadley lays down a straight flush is priceless.

After that, Hadley starts raking in winnings, and we're back to the old Hadley that I know so well. I have to fight to keep myself from smiling as I watch her. I'm proud of her, and I feel like I could watch her work all night.

But there are eyes on me.

Speaking of, it's about time to check in. I head

upstairs to the next floor, a balcony that wraps around the whole casino and provides a lovely view of a large part of the casino floor and the gamblers. It also gives the security guards a good vantage point to watch out for cheating. The ones up close and personal with the guests catch most attempts, but a bird's eye view is invaluable backup.

I make my way to one of the best seats on the floor, overlooking all of it from the back and center of this floor. Jerry is sitting there, sipping a vodka tonic and glaring down at the casino from above. My broad shouldered and bulky form draws some attention, so it isn't long before his soulless eyes flit up to me, and he gives a subtle but noticeable nod that I give back to him. It's a silent, quick signal between the two of us—all is well.

Heading to the railing, I peer down at the same floor Jerry is looking at, and I follow his gaze. Unsurprisingly, he's looking at Hadley's table, and I'd bet anything that he's checking out Hadley herself. There's a kind of hunger to his eyes that I recognize all too well. It fills me with anger and makes me want to pull my gun on him right here and now.

Of course, all that would do is get me and Hadley killed along with Jerry, and I don't plan on sharing a deathday with that son of a bitch.

Hadley's strategy inspires me, and I realize I need to take a different approach to this whole situation than just trying to stay out of the line of fire. I don't even need to think five steps ahead of the game. Like Hadley, I need to think exactly one step ahead of Jerry—it just has to be the *right* step.

I watch Jerry without looking directly at him, pretending to be watching Hadley's game from up above as she trounces her competition. He's a methodical man, even though he's vicious and driven by instinct. He wants Hadley, I know that much now. But he's been very careful about how he goes about it. He could have had her by now, if he was being direct and persistent. I have good eyes, but I don't know everything, and we're playing on Jerry's home field.

Could it be more than lust motivating him?

The way Jerry watches Hadley, I can definitely tell he's drinking in her body, but for lack of a better way of putting it, he could be making his move right now. I would be a hell of a fight to take down, but he has numbers on his side, and doesn't seem to realize I'm not on it anymore. It would be simple to grab Hadley. Why isn't he doing that?

His eyes aren't just watching her body, I realize. They're watching her game.

Whenever she makes a play that impresses him, he seems pleased. He never leans over to comment to either of his guards, which is unusual. He usually loves gossiping about the latest and best gamblers in his casino.

Then it hits me.

This is his job interview for Hadley. He isn't just interested in taking her for her body, but he wants to use her for her skills, too. A prisoner who gives him physical comfort as well as a huge source of income —she'd be perfect for him.

He wants to make sure she's as good at her game as Carl boasted she is before he makes what he sees as an investment.

All that is just a hunch that crosses my mind at first, but then I start to think over the facts. How could a man like Carl dig himself into a debt that deep that fast? I looked over the numbers, and by all rights, Carl looked like a responsible, careful man. Hell, thanks to his gamblers, he never would have gotten caught if not for Jerry nailing him on this debt.

It's no secret that a mafia debt is a fool's gamble. It's something you're forced to do, not something you choose to do, unless you're very stupid. Carl is not very stupid.

But neither is Jerry, and Jerry got where he is today by a lifelong career of stabbing people in the back to climb the ladder higher. To a man like Jerry, having a man like Carl in his debt is a very useful thing, especially knowing Carl is a coward, *and* that he has women like Hadley at his disposal to rake in obscene amounts of money with.

Better yet, Carl doesn't have any friends. Or if he does, they're nowhere near here.

All that amounts to one thing: Carl Owens is a very tempting target to utterly destroy, from Jerry's perspective. It isn't much of a reach to think that Jerry might have orchestrated this whole mess, or at least had a strong hand in guiding it.

I furrow my brow. If my hunch is right, that means we're in a much more dangerous situation than I thought. Jerry thinks he's holding all the cards in his own house, and confidence can make a man do the impossible.

My eyes flit over to Jerry, and I suddenly realize that I've been staring at Hadley too long—Jerry's seat is empty, and his guards are gone. He's on the move! I look up and start letting my gaze pan around the floor without seeming too obvious, but my heart is pounding against my chest. I'm sure part of it is just nerves after figuring out what I've just realized, but that doesn't change the fact that Jerry is a very dangerous man, and he has his eyes on Hadley.

I look back down, and I realize that Hadley is standing up too. Moreover, she's sweeping in her massive earnings and leaving the table. I clench my jaw, wishing I were down there to give her a signal. I can't contact her from up here, not without giving away what I'm trying to do.

Without another moment's hesitation, I head toward the stairs. Suddenly, I'm seeing danger everywhere. Every other enforcer who just casually crosses paths with me looks like he's about to pull a gun on me. Everyone walking vaguely my direction is about to try to take a swing at me. I fight hard to keep my composure as I move, and finally, I reach the stairs and hurry down them.

Paranoia can keep a man safe, but it can also make him foolish. I can't jump at shadows. It would give everything away.

But by the time I reach the floor, Hadley is nowhere to be seen. I curse under my breath and make my way into the crowd. Wading through the sea of expensive tailored suits and stunning dresses is simple enough, thanks to my stature, and I'd think that finding Hadley would be just as easy thanks to how distinctive she looks, but she vanished.

I start to feel adrenaline pumping through my veins. I'm not about to lose Hadley this easily. Could Jerry have had her taken the second I turned my head? No, there's no way he could have been watching me that closely, could he?

Finally, my eyes fall on neither Hadley nor Jerry, but one of the bodyguards who was with Jerry earlier. I make my way over to him, and he barely has a second to react to me before I grab him by the tie and pull him close to me.

"Where is Jerry?" I growl urgently as he staggers.

"What the fuck, Dom?" he growls back, pulling away, but I keep a grip on him.

"It's urgent," I reiterate. The guy stammers for a moment, then shakes his head as I release him.

"He went down to the security room," he says, jabbing a thumb back to the elevators. "Said he was meeting someone. What's gotten you so touchy today?"

Carl.

Without answering his question, I start making my way through the crowds to the elevators, and I slide inside, flashing my security badge at other people trying to get in before the doors slide shut and start to take me down to levels that only staff have access to.

I feel the weight of my gun at my side, not willing to let the cameras see me put my hand on it. I don't know what I'm about to walk in on, but I know there's a damn good chance it'll turn into a bloodbath.

I feel like I'm prying open the toothy maw of some ancient dragon to peer into his stomach.

I feel like I'm being interrogated by the most murderous man in the world.

I am not so egotistical and stubborn as to pretend I'm not afraid. I'm definitely afraid. In fact, I'm just about scared out of my damn mind right now. I am standing in the very belly of the beast, trapped in this tiny, buzzing room filled with camera monitors and endless keyboards and buttons.

It rather looks like a scene from some cheesy 90s flick about the Y2K scare. I know the people who work down here in this darkened, dusty, claustrophobic room must know my face by now. They are the ones who watch the screens, who stalk every winner and loser upstairs in the bustling rooms of the casino. They regard us shrewdly from below, judging and taking notes, deciding how strong or weak we are, how much of a threat we pose to the way of the world here in this microcosm.

Everything is shoved in together, the rights and wrongs and cosmic karma and great odysseys for money and pride, balled up into a tight fist. The casino is a clenched hand, a pressure cooker in which people at the ends of their old money ropes or on their first big new money spending spree. Everything is intensified by a thousand here. Everyone is under scrutiny, all the time, whether the eyes that watch us are visible to us or not.

Down here lives the oculus. This is where they watch us.

I'm standing under the grim, flickering light of a single bulb dangling from the ceiling. It's a stark contrast to the wealth and luxury of the upper floors. Who knew that underneath the pomp and opulence of the casino floor there lay a dungeon-like chamber of pale, weary watchers?

Right now, though, all the people who usually work down here have been rushed out. I don't know where they went, but when the door closes solidly behind me, I realize with a twinge of fear that I am all alone with Jerry Laskin. That is by design, of course. He wants me alone. He wants me vulnerable, off my game. He's going to try and intimidate me into giving him whatever it is he thinks he wants from me. An apology? Probably not. He's clearly not the kind of man who needs to hear "I'm sorry." A confession? Most likely. Jerry will want to trick me into admitting exactly how I've been winning all these games.

But that's not all he will want from me. I am no fool. He wants more than my admission of guilt, of how I've been using the power of psychology and counting cards to walk away with his money. He will want to punish me. I don't know what sort of penal system he has etched out in his dark mind but I know it's got to be something terrible. He doesn't strike me as an especially forgiving man. And winning his money is possibly the greatest and most egregious sin I could possibly commit against him.

Men like Laskin—like Carl Owens—live for the money. He lives to see those dollar signs rolling in. It's his obsession, his lifeblood. It's what keeps him moving forward, his sole motivation outside of spite. Those are dangerous fixations, but he has clearly learned how to avoid taking the punishments for himself. He's got an unending parade of lackeys and fallback guys to take the hit. He outsources his pain, his losses.

The winner takes all, and he always wins. But not this time. Not with me in the building. No matter how corrupt he is, no matter the kinds of criminal maneuvers he uses to get ahead, he can never compete with my ability to smash the competition.

I'm an enigma to him, and I can see a shining glint of curiosity in his beady black eyes as he looks at me. But I am first and foremost a threat, and that fact takes precedence over all else.

"I believe a congratulations may be in order here, yes?" he says finally, his voice every bit as gruff and gravelly as his appearance.

I force a coquettish giggle and bite my lip. I feel my cheeks start to flush slightly rosy pink. Perfect. Just as planned. This is my angle.

"Luck must be my lady tonight," I remark with a playful shrug. "I just can't believe it."

"Hmm," Laskin grunts, nodding very slowly. "I can't believe it either."

"Pardon me, but you said something about a VIP suite, and this doesn't exactly look like any kind of suite at all," I point out. I bat my eyelashes subtly and grace him with a smile.

"You're right. This is not the suite I promised. This is, ah, a pit stop on the way, if you will. I hope that doesn't bother you," he says quietly, that false smile still plastered uncomfortably on his ugly mug.

"Oh, of course not," I tell him with a wave of my hand. "No problem."

"I just have some... questions. For the big winner," he notes, his smile looking more and more sharklike as it remains frozen on his face.

"Ah. Well, in that case, ask away," I reply cheerily. It's important that I don't show fear.

"I'm looking to expand, you know. Broaden my, ah, portfolio, if you will. Is that something you can relate to?" he asks rather cryptically.

I frown. "I'm sorry. I don't follow," I lie.

Jerry licks his lips, staring me up and down for a moment. He steps closer, and I can feel his rancid breath on my body. I don't move. I hold my ground. It's all I have. He could so easily break me in half…

Just then, the door swings open with a bang and we both look over at the doorway in shock. My heart skips a beat when my eyes meet his—it's Dominick! Somehow he's managed to find me. I stare at him with wide eyes, wondering what the hell he's got planned. Laskin is every bit as confused and startled, and I can see an angry twitch working in his jaw.

"You're interrupting something very important here, Dominick," Laskin snarls.

"My apologies, sir. But there's been a security breach I needed to inform you of. It's serious. All hands on deck. Thought you might like to be made aware of the situation," Dom rattles off matter-of-factly. Laskin tenses up, looking back and forth between Dom and me. I can tell he's reluctant to leave me now.

Finally, though, he groans and snaps his fingers to beckon Dom into the room. "Take my place. Watch over our esteemed VIP winner for me while I go take care of business," he ordered Dominick. "I won't be gone long. Oh, and remember to treat our guest here with... respect."

He winks at Dominick and then slips out of the room. Dom immediately shuts the door and rushes over to me, grabbing both of my hands tightly in his. There's a bright fire flashing in his gorgeous eyes.

"How did you find me?" I ask in a hushed tone.

He shakes his head. "Never mind that. It's not important. Right now, I need you to listen to what I have to say. Okay? Can you do that for me?" he asks fervently.

I frown at him, a little offended. "Yes, Dom. I know how to listen. I'm not a child."

"Good. Then prove it. I have a lot to say. First of all, you know my boss Jerry Laskin, that man who brought you down here," he began.

"Yes. We've met. He's... enchanting," I say acidically.

Dom gives me a warning glance and I sigh, pretending to zip my lips closed.

"Hadley, he's been watching you. This is bigger than just some debt collection. Especially after the way you swept the competition tonight. You're a prime target. This is why they haven't taken you yet. Because of your ability to play. Carl didn't offer you up just to... clear his debts. Or at least, not the way you thought. He wants you to play for him, and he's not going to take no for an answer," Dominick says grimly.

"Dom, I figured that much out on my own. Why do you think I came back here?"

"Hadley, no. This is bigger than either of us realized. He wants you to help him with this massive hostile takeover plot, and I can tell you from personal experience that he will use whatever methods possible to get you there. Not one of those methods is gentle," he explains, glancing toward the door.

"We don't have much time, do we?" I ask, knowing the security breach was a lie. He nods.

"Exactly," he says. "We need to move quickly. I don't know what he wants, but—"

"A massive hostile takeover that he needs a solid winner for? Dom, he's going to be trying to take on the other casinos. Jerry Laskin wants to weaponize us. He wants to use us to take down the casinos one by one, lower their defenses, make them vulnerable. But why?"

"So that he can swoop in and take them for his own, at a very discounted price," Dom says darkly.

"Like some fucked-up game of Monopoly," I sigh. "Shit. What an asshole."

"Yeah, well, the mafia is made up almost entirely of assholes, you'll find," he replies.

"Except you," I clarify, looking at him sidelong. He smiles softly.

"Don't count me out just yet. I may not be as downright evil as some of my colleagues but I think the title of 'asshole' still suits me pretty damn well. But either way, we're both going to be assholes if Laskin pulls this off. You'll be tied to the mafia, too. You've dealt in high-risk and danger before, but this... this would be an entirely different animal, Hadley," he warns.

"We have to do something," I murmur to myself. Then I suddenly look up at him with round, bright eyes. "This is going to be risky, but... Dom, I have an idea, and you're not going to like it."

Just as she's about to tell me, the elevator beeps outside our room, and the door slams open.

DOMINICK

That was bad, and leaving Hadley behind is even worse, but we have no choice.

I have to trust that she can handle herself in there, alone, with Jerry. Deep down, I know she can. She's more skilled at just about everything than most people give her credit for, and I know she can handle herself in this situation.

She said she had a plan, though. Something that would be risky. Something that I wouldn't like. Before she could tell me, though, Jerry walked in, red faced and annoyed. It was lucky for me that one of the other enforcers had just caught a big cheat Jerry was on the lookout for, so my lie wasn't exposed.

But now she's alone with him, and I have to trust that she'll be getting out of that room. If Jerry wants her to be able to gamble for him, he's going to try to butter her up, first. Offer her a deal she can't refuse.

It won't be until later he'll start using other measures to keep her in line.

That doesn't make it any easier for me to leave her in the dragon's den with the boss himself, though. I hate having to leave things in someone else's hands. I always have.

The most I can do right now is try to keep up contact with her as soon as she gets out of there, and tell myself that she *will* get out of there.

Earlier this morning, I remember someone clearing out of one of the VIP suites on the upper floors. I don't want cameras to see me heading to Hadley's room too often, so I decide to try to commandeer this one. I head to the elevators and ride it all the way up to the uppermost floors, where the real money stays. I head to the room in question and see a maid just finishing up inside, pushing her cart out. She looks at me, then looks scared for a moment as I approach, putting a finger to my lips.

"You never saw me here," I say quietly as I slip her a $50 and use my card key to open the door. "And nobody will bother me in here for the next few hours, understand?"

"Yes, of course, sir," she says hurriedly, and she bustles away, leaving me in peace with the room. I head inside and text Hadley the room number and nothing more, hoping she picks up on the message.

I pace around, thinking things over, waiting for Hadley to make it up to me and reassuring myself that she'll be here. I never rely on anyone unless I'm positive they're going to pull through, and god, do I need Hadley to pull through for me.

We've both been jerked around for too long by too many people. Beating the shit out of Carl felt good, but it's a bitter feeling in hindsight, knowing I was just softening him up and intimidating him for a bigger plot Jerry is masterminding. And I know Hadley has been chafing under Carl for so long that she must be itching to be rid of him. The only thing I don't know is whether she'll be willing to cross that necessary line to do what needs to be done.

God knows I'm long past that line with Jerry. I'll pull that trigger without a second thought.

I wait for what feels like an hour, or maybe several hours. Finally, I hear a knock at the door. Instinctively, my hand goes to my gun, and I approach the door silently, every muscle in my body tense. If Jerry got to Hadley, then there could be a whole group of enforcers waiting to storm in the door and take me down in an instant. If that happened, I was going to give them hell, but that wouldn't do shit to help Hadley.

I reach the door and look through the peephole to see Hadley standing there. I know there's a chance there still may be others around the corner, waiting to slip in after I open the door, but Hadley looks confident—more confident than I figure she would if she were a hostage like that.

So, I finally open the door, hand still on my gun.

Hadley forces her way in immediately and slides her arms around my neck, then presses her lips to mine as she pushes the door shut behind me and latches it locked.

She melts into my arms as I wrap my free hand around her waist and pull her close to me, and our moans run together as I walk her back against the wall and pin her against it.

"I take it things went better than I worried," I growl into her ear once our lips finally separate with a wet sound.

"I never disappoint," she purrs. "You know that by now."

"That's what I love about you," I growl. "Now tell me the plan."

"Later," she says, her mouth covering mine and I slide my fingers into her hair and take a firm grip.

I pull her hair back and expose her neck, letting me put my mouth to it and suck on the soft skin. I can smell her perfume on her like pheromones, and it drives me wild. I move her body around and start walking her back toward the massive bed in the luxurious suite. As soon as we reach the edge, I push her down onto it.

We start stripping without even thinking about it. Our shoes come off, her gloves fall to the floor, my jacket hits the sofa, she slides my tie off me, and I help her out of that elaborate dress. The adrenaline is spiked between both of us, the risk of her plan making everything seem more urgent. We're walking the plank to our deaths, and I'll be damned if I'm not going to go out smelling like her.

I'm dressed well, but Hadley is always stunning. Taking her ensemble apart always feels almost sacrilegious, like I'm defiling something precious. And part of me thinks she likes that.

Soon, we're both naked, and I can feel all the tension and desire that's been building up in me suddenly boiling over. I descend on her, gripping her hips and bringing my mouth to her left nipple and start ravishing it. I bring as much as her breast into my mouth as I can, playing with her stiff nipple with my tongue and groping the other with a strong, firm hand. She gasps, desperate for my touch even as she squirms away from me.

I sit up on the bed and turn her around, sitting her in my lap and reaching around her hips to finger her with my left hand while my right touches her breast and my lips brush against her neck.

"I've been waiting for this all day," I growl.

"That makes two of us," she whispers back, but I cut her off at the last syllable by slipping my fingers deeper into her and playing with her. She twists and squirms, but I keep her pinned against me as I start stroking gently, feeling the warmth and wetness of her folds the more I explore them. I push my hips up and grind my cock between her ass cheeks as I finger her, and I know she's getting her own thrill out of the feeling of my cock pulsing with need for her.

It doesn't take her long to get wet enough for me to enter her. I bring my fingers out of her pussy and up to my lips, and she shivers with pleasure before I hoist her up by the hips. I let her wet pussy feel the bulging crown of my cock that sticks straight up toward her, and she arches her back instinctively as I lower her onto me.

The dark, bulging tip of my cock grinds against the front of her inner walls, and the shiver of delight I feel from her whole body is like nothing else in the world. She's hot, wet, and soft, and my rough hands reward her with long, loving strokes along her smooth inner thighs. I start pushing my hips up and bouncing her on my cock, and it takes her no time to find a rhythm with me.

She rolls her shoulders back and leans against my broad chest, feeling my warmth and muscle all around her. I keep my hands on her breasts, flicking and gently pinching her swollen nipples while I feel her get slicker on my cock with each new thrust. I start almost panting, letting out sharp, hot breaths as I rut up into her, and that seems to have an effect. She starts gasping for air along with my rutting, and I can see her blush growing out of the corner of my eye.

I bring my hands down to her hips and hold

them, pinning her to me, and at the same time, I start rutting up into her harder and faster. I forget that we're making love and turn to pure, raw aggression. I fuck her hard from below, wanting to tease out that peak that I know is just around the corner.

And just as expected, a moment later, Hadley's hands go to my thighs, scratching me on her way to the sheets. She grabs handfuls of them and braces herself as my relentless thrusting drives her to orgasm, and she lets out a sharp cry as she does. I slide a hand over her mouth and silence her while she comes, and I keep thrusting up, never giving her a moment's break until she's finished.

Once she is, I use my arms to carefully twist us around and put her on her knees on the bed. I push her forward until she's on her hands and knees, and I grab her hips again to start fucking her from behind.

I notice Hadley's hair is strewn over her face, so I reach down and gather it up, wrapping it around my fist like a leash and pulling her back until her whole back arches. The sound of her desperate gasping is music to my ears. Each time I thrust into her, I feel my powerful body pulsing with desire, more than ready to release into her. My balls are swollen and heavy, and I'm eager to let my load blow into her...but not yet.

My hips pound into her so long that she almost collapses on the bedsheets. She scrambles to grab a pillow and hug it as she lets her face get planted into the sheets while I pull her back, holding her tight against me as I abuse her tight pussy. It fills her so completely that I can feel everything, every little twinge and change in her, each one giving both of us unending pleasure.

She bites down on the pillow moments before she lets out what would have been a loud, desperate moan as she comes again, and I hold her hips tightly, possessively, greedily hoarding her for myself as pleasure washes over her entire form.

But this time, she seems genuinely worn out, so I slow down, taking it just a little easier on her as I guide her through the orgasm. I massage her insides with my cock until it's over, and after that, I slide out of her carefully and turn her around, laying her down on her back.

She looks up at me absolutely dizzy, panting for breath as I slide my cock back into her from the top. She closes her eyes and shudders in delight as I enter her, but this time, I bend down and kiss her.

For a few moments, I go gently with her, assuming she's worn out. I move my cock back and forth, glancing down and seeing its thick girth appear and vanish through those wet lips over and over again. But as I'm doing that, I notice her start to push her hips up, and she pulls her legs back to drape over my thick shoulders.

"Come in me," she dares me through gritted

teeth. I look at her blushing face, so full of determination and desire. "Don't hold anything back."

I can sense the unspoken words just behind her lips.

This could be our last time together.

I lift her hips up to angle her up, and from there onward, I give her what she wants. I start thrusting into her from this new angle, feeling new sensations ripple up my body and make my balls tighten and beg me for release with each thrust. I hold out so, so long, pounding into her and hearing our wet slapping fill the room that belongs to some other rich fuck who's going to feel our lovemaking in the air.

I watch her whole body get thrusted back each time I push into her, and even so worn out and vanquished as she is, she pushes up and works with me. She starts clenching her pussy, urging me to release, and finally, I start to let myself go.

I feel a spurt of precum escape me as the tightness in my shaft starts to unwind bit by bit, and in the next thrust, I feel myself jolt over the point of no return. I completely lose the practiced rhythm and descend into wild, primal rutting that makes her gasp and pant as I bring my mouth to her neck and ravish her. I pin her arms to the bed at the wrists, and I feel my hot, white seed burst into her.

I let out a long groan as shot after shot releases into her. At the same time, I feel her honey flooding my shaft as she comes, and we buck into each other with untamed ferocity until we're completely, utterly spent.

Finally, it's just the two of us and the sounds of our panting filling the large room as we stare into each other's eyes.

I slowly slide out of Hadley, feeling the last few pulses of unbridled pleasure ripple from my shaft up through the rest of my body, and I watch the thin trail of white run from her nether lips once I'm out of her. I lie down next to her and let out a deep, ragged breath, staring at those beautiful eyes, that glowing, satisfied face on the silk sheets as she watches me.

"That right there," I say, nodding to her, "that's why we deserve better than this."

"Because we fuck so good?" she teases me, propping herself up on an elbow and batting her long eyelashes at me temptingly. I chuckle and lean forward to kiss her.

"Yes," I say, "but I mean, what we have. You're in a whole higher league than the likes of Carl, just like I'm a cut above Jerry. We don't need either of them. We're making something... so fucking beautiful together," I say, looking up and down her body. "We could run this city, if it were up to us. We just need to figure out how to get up there, and slipping around their backs forever isn't going to cut it."

"My plan might be able to... take care of that."

"Why don't we discuss it over a shower?" I

suggest, nodding back to the large bathroom.

"Is this even a room you have checked out?" she asks, laughing as I reach down and take her hands to pull her out of bed and up to her feet.

"No," I admit, "so someone could walk in on us at basically any time, but they can fuck off. What we're doing right now is more important."

"I like the way you think," she says with a smile.

Moments later, we're in a bathroom that's quickly filling up with hot steam and stepping into the shower, letting hot water soak and cleanse our naked bodies. I feel the water run through my short hair, and the moment drops of water start to patter on her immaculate face, I want to push her up against the cool glass and fuck her all over again.

Instead, I content myself to turn her around and hug her from behind, resting my cock against her ass and feeling it pulse softly while we rock back and forth together.

"So, what's this plan of yours?" I ask.

"Well, if we want to run things the way we want to," she says, "it won't do to just deal with Carl and Jerry. We need something bigger than that."

"You're right," I say. "There are too many people still loyal to him. He holds a lot of sway with... well, the entire casino. These are mafia politics we're talking about. We can't just go in all guns blazing."

"No guns blazing, in fact," she says, surprising me. But the look on her face shows just how pleased she is with the idea, and she goes on smoothly. "We've got the easiest way to make Jerry Laskin look bad sitting right in front of us: catch him cheating."

"At what?"

"At one big game between him and Carl, winner takes all," she says smugly. "I convince Carl that I'll go peacefully *and* hand over Vanessa to Jerry as the cherry on top. But I want him to put us up as part of the pot. Winner takes all, and Jerry has to win us, fair and square. At a public game."

"So, if Carl wins, he keeps you and Vanessa *and* doesn't have to pay his debt back, and if Jerry wins, he gets you both and every penny Carl's got."

"Exactly," Hadley says, turning to look up at me.

"You know Jerry would just kill Carl if he lost, right?"

"Yes, and that doesn't matter one bit," she says. "Because security is going to catch Jerry cheating at his own rigged game."

"And what idiot in his right mind would dare call out Jerry Laskin for cheating in his own casino?" I ask. I know I sound like an asshole, but I've got to make sure her plan is completely airtight in every possible way. But as always, Hadley impresses, and she looks good while doing so.

"Easy," she says as if waiting for that question. "I know a security guard who Vanessa has wrapped around her finger. He'd do anything to make sure she's safe, but Jerry doesn't know that."

"Impressive," I say, stroking her sides and massaging her hips. "Last but not least, what makes you think Jerry will cheat in the first place? What if he plays straight and takes Carl to the cleaners?"

"That is a risk," she admits, "but Jerry wants me. You probably saw how he was looking at me from up above. My guess is they'll both be cheating, but Carl cut his teeth counting cards when he was in his twenties. He's a good cheater, and less likely to get caught at it if we have our man watching Jerry instead. And if a mobster wants something bad enough, he'll do anything for it."

"You learn that from watching me?" I tease, slipping my finger between her legs and rubbing it over her clit. She gasps, but she lets out a soft laugh as she leans back against me.

"Maybe," she says. "This is the only way I can think of getting out of this without bloodshed. Without me having to run from the mafia for the rest of my life. Without having to run from you. From this."

"I like it," I admit, smiling down at her. "Just one problem—get the two bosses on board for it."

She turns around and looks at me with those eyes that show me every ounce of cunning she has, and a smile that tells me just how willing she is to use it.

"Leave that to me."

It is so silent in this basement room of the casino building that you could hear a pin drop. I'm pretty certain everyone can hear the irritating thump-thump of my heart as I stand stock-still and frozen, watching the game being set up in front of me.

There are not a lot of people here. Only a small audience of those who are intrinsically involved. Those of us who are tied to the match. Still, it should be enough.

A couple of the attendees are playing security, meant to be referees and guides, to keep the ball in center court rather than letting the high-strung, high-stakes boundaries crumble and fall. Some of them are here to watch the head of the casino bet big. And still others of us, the less fortunate few, are here because we're the prize. We're the trophy. We're the collective stack of plastic chips meant to be traded for wealth and success and ego.

Once again, I find myself playing the role of some powerful man's toy. Both of them want me, for similar selfish reasons. At one end of the table sits my current boss, the man who has controlled me like a puppet for years now: Carl. He's leaned back in his fancy, expensive chair, wearing his fancy, expensive clothes and cologne so thick it burns my nostrils from way over here. There is a smug but rather pinched smile on his broad face, his eyes lidded as though he's just the calmest, coolest cucumber in the crisper.

But that's all for show. It's all part of his ruse. I have been at this industry far long enough to recognize a play when I see one. And this is all on purpose. The way he sits jaunty in his chair. The way he clicks two plastic chips against each other to make an annoying noise that grates on everyone's nerves, including his opponent.

Speaking of whom, his opponent is no novice to this world, either.

Because Carl is playing against the one man who could possibly threaten his livelihood to such a screaming-high level: Jerry Laskin.

At one end of the table is my boss, and at the other end is Dominick's boss. The two of them have wildly different approaches to this match. While Carl is trying to play it cool, wearing that smug smirk on his stupid face, Jerry is going for intimidation. And with his heavy jowls, the purplish-gray bags under his drooping black eyes, the perpetual frown lines carved into his rough-looking face, and his overall aura of beastlike predation, he's pulling it off pretty damn well.

He looks rather like some grizzled old bloodhound, and there's a haunted look to his features that make everyone uneasy, instantly.

They're both gambling tonight to win me, as if I were a prize, and not a flesh and blood woman with wants and needs and desires of my own. As if I were simply a stack of chips, meant to be passed around and turned in for cash.

The room we're all in is impressive, not the grimy, glum, dusty basement one might imagine would exist underneath a casino. It's fully-finished with glitzy mid-century-modern fixtures and furniture. There's a chandelier of sparkling Tiffany glass dangling over the center of the card table, serving as the sole source of light for the entire great room. It illuminates the glossy, unscratched mahogany table beneath it, with its elegantly carved table legs and side beveling. On the walls of the room are several evenly-spaced triangular sconces, but they're unlit. At least I can say one thing positive about our respective bosses: they sure can appreciate what it takes to create a moody ambiance.

And it wasn't easy to get them here, either. I have

always been a very persuasive woman. Ever since I was a little girl, I've been teaching myself and finding new ways to convince people to do what I want. It's a skill I've worked hard to hone and perfect over the years, and it's saved my ass on multiple occasions. Of course, being an attractive woman certainly helps in that arena. All I have to do is bat my lashes, giggle, twirl my hair, bite my lip, lean in close, whisper, walk with undulating purpose —it's all part of the same winning package.

Even Carl, who has known me for years, who helped build me into the treacherous competitor I am today, is not immune to my forces. Dominick, too, is very convincing, but not in the same way. I use my wiles, and he uses his strength. I can con, but he can control. Together, we admittedly make one hell of a dynamic and dangerous couple.

And so it was with his assistance that we managed to convince our respective bosses to sit down for a glamorous, winner takes all card game. As it turns out, it's less difficult to coerce a couple of lifelong thrill-seekers and gamblers to take on a match like this. We knew they would each underestimate their opponent's skill and desire. Their egos will be their downfalls.

It's a wild bet, but they agreed to it as a means of resolving their longtime stand-off. As long as they stayed at odds, neither of them could move forward. This card game is designed to break the stalemate.

On top of that, it's Jerry's best chance of getting the girls—Vanessa and me—and Carl's only shot at surviving past this debt to the mafia he's incurred.

Dominick urged Jerry to play under the conditions that if he wins, all of Carl's girls will gladly and peacefully go to work for him instead. Carl will still have his debts to pay. And if that is the case, then I know Carl will die. The mafia won't let him live in the red forever. If they can't exorcise the money out of him, they will make him pay with blood. Perhaps there is a part of me somewhere deep down that might be capable of feeling sorry for him. After all, Carl has been a part of my life for a long, long time now. But when I think of all the terrible things he has done, not only to me, but to others… well, it's hard to feel anything for him but hatred.

I convinced Carl to play with the promise that if he wins, his debts to the mafia, to Jerry himself, will be cleared.

Dominick and I put my plan into motion, and it's nearly flawless. Except for something that Carl requested on top of having his debts cleared.

He asked for security footage to be destroyed. He wouldn't tell me what was on it, but Dominick was able to fill in the blanks. He tracked down the tape. At first, he didn't even want to tell me what was on it, but that was not an option.

Seeing it for myself was something I wish I could take back, though.

Carl, grabbing Vanessa's wrist. Pushing her against the wall. Hurting her.

Evidence that he was the one who assaulted Vanessa the night she called me.

She never told me who it was, and now I know why. She was terrified, not because it was some random casino creep, but because it was the man who held her life in his hands. It's no wonder she went missing right after that. He must have been worried that she was going to tell someone about what he did and had her kidnapped. But if he could do something like that, knowing his rival would have it on tape, then I'm terrified to think of what he's capable of in private.

There's no way he's going to win tonight. Neither of them will.

They just don't know it yet.

"Where's the other girl?" Jerry asks, looking at me, and then scanning the crowd for Vanessa. The other woman he's betting for.

"Don't worry," Carl says with a smooth, practiced grin. "Once you win, Hadley and her will be yours. Hadley will see to that," he promises and hatred fills my veins. But things have to go as planned, so I nod at Jerry.

"She's laying low, but I know where to find her."

Jerry scowls a bit at that answer, looking at Carl angrily.

"This is bad business, Carl. I thought we were past that."

"Well she got spooked after your boys roughed her up."

"Is that what happened?" Jerry asked, raising a brow, and Carl stares at him, stony as ever. The game hasn't even started, but they're both bluffing each other.

All around the room, pacing and stalking like some sharp-eyed jungle predator, is Dominick. He's keeping watch, playing security to this high-stakes, illegal game. His eyes see everything. His training is absolute, his control over the situation so measured. Nothing will slip past him, and I know it. In fact, I can almost convince myself I'm safe here, having Dom only a few feet away. He's like a guardian angel for me. Whenever he's close, I'm damn near invincible. I glance across the room at him and we lock eyes for a moment. There's not a flicker of a changed expression between us, but I can see in his eyes an agreement. An understanding. Our plan is set in motion, and now all we have to do is watch the game.

A stoic, quiet older man I recognize as one of the dealers from upstairs deals their cards out and steps back. There is utter silence in the room as the game begins. We all watch with rapt attention, learning Carl and Jerry's respective maneuvers and tactics. Carl continues to smile and play it casual. Jerry remains stone-cold and brooding. With every card laid down, with every reveal, every bluff, a titter of awe and wonder passes through the small crowd watching. I do my best to follow the numbers, counting in my head frantically. It doesn't matter much who wins, but I need to stay on top of things either way.

The game tilts in the favor of Jerry Laskin.

He's winning, and that stony look on his face starts to crack, letting a smile sneak through. I stare at him with suspicion, and he catches my eye, a smug look of satisfaction and lust crossing his features. Something is off.

Carl knows it, too. He looks nervous now, for once.

But then, the young security guard comes over and murmurs in the dealer's ear. The dealer raises a brow, terror seeming to drain all color from his face. The security guard—the enforcer who is sweet on Vanessa—remains stoic. He nods at the dealer, urging him on.

The dealer swallows, and I can see the gears turning in his head, wondering at the consequences of revealing what was just told to him.

"Jerry Laskin has been cheating," the dealer grumbles, pointing an accusing finger.

Gasps and arguments break out through the room and some of Carl's guys start to hulk toward

Jerry, cracking their knuckles and scowling with rage.

"I knew it," Carl says, shaking his head and sighing. "I knew you just couldn't play clean if you wanted to. Dirty, cheating bastard."

"I don't know what you're talking about," Jerry growls, looking at the young man who just sold him out, hatred in his eyes.

"Come on, give it up!" snaps one of the security guys, looking at Jerry with frustration.

Carl raises a hand, a rather worrying look of intrigue on his face. "No, no. Let's not cause any trouble over this. My opponent may feel intimidated by me to the point of stooping to cheat. I can understand that. I do have that effect on others sometimes," he says smugly.

"Oh, can it, you slimy weasel," grunts Jerry.

"In fact," Carl says, interrupting his opponent, "as a show of good sportsmanship and confidence, I will continue the game, despite my enemy's inability to play it straight. But there's a catch. If you're going to cheat, then it's only fair I pull my own trump card, as well."

There's no sound as we all wait breathlessly for his next words.

Carl slowly stands up and brushes off his suit, looking at Jerry with a raised eyebrow.

"Not even your dishonest ways will stand up to

my secret weapon," he says, then turns to look at me, to my horror. "You will play my protege. Hadley."

I'm speechless, staring at my boss in shock. I can't move. This isn't how it was supposed to go.

"Come along, sweetheart. The game is still going. Don't make us wait," Carl chirps, ushering me into his chair. I can't refuse. My own life is on the table.

I make brief eye contact with a rather puzzled and concerned Dom as I slide into the seat and scoot up to the table. Jerry looks much more relaxed now than before. It's easy to see why. Not only is he being allowed to continue playing despite getting caught red-handed cheating, but now he's facing a *woman*. I can tell he underestimates me. Immediately. But that's his downfall. My boss may be a good player, but he's got nothing on me.

And Jerry learns that very quickly. Maybe he thought watching me for a single game was enough to *know* me, to be able to head me off, but he's dead wrong. The game takes a turn. I win hand after hand, eliciting muffled gasps and cheers from the crowd. The smile hovering on Jerry's face is fading, downturning further with every loss. Before long, I've got the game in the bag. Jerry's skills are dwarfed by mine. Even with the nervousness prickling in my veins, I'm in control here.

"I can't believe it," Jerry mutters roughly to himself, eyes bugging.

"You lost," Carl says gleefully, clapping his hands.

"How wonderful! I knew my Hadley would never let me down. You see now what you'll be missing out on! To think, I might've lost my girls to you. Do you understand what an asset the girl is? And she's still mine. How lovely."

"You must have cheated somehow," Jerry shouts, standing up abruptly. His chair is knocked aside as he stands there fuming and panting, his eyes glaring at Carl with venom. His hands ball into fists. "I won't let you win," he snaps, reaching for the gun he had stowed at his spine. But before he can even get there, the air is split with a deafening CRACK!

Everyone screams and ducks down, reacting to the gunshot. And when the reverberations calm down just enough, I turn to see Carl recocking his gun with a big grin on his face. On the floor lies the body of Jerry Laskin, his head crowned with a spreading pool of bright red blood. Carl just killed a man! In his own club! In front of a crowd of witnesses.

And, to my horror, Dom is nowhere in sight.

"Well, it's been fun," Carl says lightly, running toward the exit with his gun pointed outward. The security guards all fall back with their arms up in surrender, the crowd making a wide berth for him to pass through.

"No!" I shout, feeling our carefully-laid plans slipping through my fingers right in front of me. It can't end this way. It just can't. I make a dive for the exit, tripping over Jerry's corpse and careening into the wall beside the door. Carl gives me a look of pure loathing and hastily grabs me, yanking me to his chest and pressing the cold barrel of his gun against my temple. I can scarcely breathe for fear, my eyes wide and searching for someone to save me.

"Now! You will all stand back and let me leave, and if anyone tries to stop me, I will put a bullet right through this brilliant, beautiful head here," Carl announces, tapping my temple with the end of the barrel.

I whimper, feeling my legs start to tingle and go numb as mortal terror grips my entire body. This is the end. It has to be. All my clever calculations of risk and rewards, my understanding of psychology and why people act the way they do, my manipulation of events and circumstances all just crumbles away.

I made a bad call.

Slowly, Carl turns to open the door to escape, still gripping me in his arms. I know I have only one last shot. If I'm going to die, I'm going to die fighting, not later on after some extended period as a hostage. So I summon up my bravery and strength and twist my body around just far enough to knee Carl in the balls. He grunts with pain and glares at me, a bright fire of loathing lit up in his eyes.

"You little bitch," he snarls. This is the end. I know it.

But in a flash of color and sound, something hits him with enough force to make him drop me to the floor. I fall down with a cry of surprise, whipping my head around just in time to see the gun fall out of Carl's hands. In a split-second reflex, I catch the piece before it hits the ground. Just a moment later, before I can figure out what's even going on, Carl's body is the next thing to fall. He lands awkwardly, facedown with his legs all bent, and I know instantaneously that he is dead.

I look up with wide eyes and a trembling chin to see Dom looming over me, his powerful chest rising and falling heavily. He wipes his hands on his pants and spits on the broken body on the floor.

"You—you killed him," Hadley whispers breathlessly as he I take her hand, pulling her to her feet.

"I did. For Vanessa. For you. For all the women he's ever hurt and all the women he was intending to hurt. You're free now, Hadley."

She stares at me, and beneath her carefully practiced facade of calm and collected, I see something lingering in her eyes. Relief. Something she's been terrified to admit to me, to herself, but she knew the risk if either of those men won. They weren't going to let her ever walk away from them. She knew too much.

And Hadley knew it. She was always going to be the ace in their back pocket.

We're done being played at a game we've mastered.

Bullets start flying, but I put my gun away—this isn't a war I'm starting, it's a coup.

We just need to get out of here alive. The fire is coming from Carl's bodyguards, and I can hear some of the other security enforcers in the casino firing back, but I only have one thing on my mind: get us out of here.

I take Hadley by the hand and run with her as fast as we can move, keeping low and weaving our way to an exit one of my associates has ready for me. In the blink of an eye, we're out of the casino floor and winding our way through the back halls. The sounds of gunfire get more distant as we hurry down to the parking garage.

"Are your men in position?" Hadley asks me through panting breaths as we run.

"Hell of a time to ask," I can't help but chuckle as we move through the hallways that I've used for ages with the other security personnel. "Yeah, unless we're about to run into a trap, we're good to go."

"And if we are?"

In response, I take out my gun and keep it at the ready as we get to the elevator leading down to the parking garage.

But when the doors slide open a few moments later, I'm greeted by the exact sight I had arranged: a valet and two enforcers standing beside Jerry's own armored limousine, door open and waiting for our escape.

"I hear gunfire," one of the enforcers says as we rush to the limo. "Is it done?"

"Yeah," I say, giving him a curt nod as Hadley hops into the vehicle. "Jerry's dead. Carl's dead. All their deals are dead. It's just us now. Cover our asses on our way out, and when we get back, you'll be rewarded for it."

He nods, and I return it before climbing into the limo with Hadley, and we pull off.

With the partition closed, Hadley and I ride in silence for a few long minutes, sitting opposite each other and breathing heavily. Finally, my face breaks into a smile, and Hadley can't help but do the same. The next moment, we start laughing, and I feel like I'm walking on clouds.

"It feels wrong to be laughing right now," Hadley says, even though she can't keep the grin off her face.

"Maybe," I say, moving over to her side of the limo and wrapping my arm around her, hugging her tight to me and kissing her on the cheek. "But I think we've earned the right to laugh whenever we want."

"I've worked through a lot of elaborate plans," she says with a wistful sigh, "but never thought I'd succeed in making one like that work."

"You don't give yourself nearly enough credit," I say, smirking. "Did you have any trouble on your end?"

"Not half as much as I expected," she says, leaning back and crossing her legs. "Just like we planned, I tipped off Carl to let him know that Jerry was going to have him killed regardless of how this game worked out, and he believed me when I told him I'd rather work for him than Jerry. And we obviously know that Carl found the gun you planted for him in his room."

"Not my best breaking and entering, but it got the job done," I say modestly. "Give a desperate man the means to undo himself, and he does all the work for you."

"The strangest thing is that part of me wants to feel bad about it," she says with a soft smile that soon fades. "But not after what we found out about him doing to Vanessa. If that's how he treats us, then there's no way it wasn't part of a pattern—Vanessa wasn't the first of us he'd abused, I'm positive about that. All the people who left his team... I just figured it was a risky life, and too much travel. There's always turnover in this line of work. I feel so blind. I didn't see it at all..."

"It was easier than I worried to get some of the other enforcers on my page," I say. "There are going to be a few messes to clean up, but that game we played is every bit as much the last nail in his coffin as the bullet was."

"So, what happens now?" Hadley asks. "Is anything stopping us from carrying out the rest of the plan?"

"Stepping in to fill the power vacuum, get the

girls back together, and use Carl's methods to bank-rupt every other hotel in the area for us to buy out?" I say, cocking my head to the side with a wicked smile. "The idea of leaving Vegas in chaos is tempting, but no, nothing's stopping us. What do you say, partner?"

I run my hand through Hadley's hair and take a gentle grip on it, tilting her head back and leaning in close, breathing up her neck and feeling her shiver as a blush comes to her face.

"Want to play the long game with me?" I whisper into her ear.

"Forever," she purrs back.

I can't hold myself back. We've been skirting with danger the entire time that we've known each other, even plunging headlong into it. Now, it's no differ-ent. I can't resist her, whether we're alone in a hotel room or in a getaway car after killing one of the most powerful men in Nevada. She's mine, and I want to show her that.

My lips press against her neck, and I breathe in the fragrant perfume she wears. I can smell it with my cologne, and it makes my heart beat faster. My hands reach over and grope her body through the staggeringly expensive dress.

I feel her soft skin and the rich fabric covering it, and it makes my cock swell in my pants. My teeth brush against her neck, sharp edges against smooth softness, and I want to bite her. Something primal and possessive is slowly awakening in me, pushing away every other instinct I have except the one to take Hadley and make her mine, as if she already isn't. I can taste that in the air, like a pheromone. We belong to each other, even here in the middle of the storm.

My arms tighten around her, and I hug her to me. While I feel her body pressing against mine, I feel one of her hands wandering up my leg toward the growing shaft below my belt. Those hands have been so skillful, so subtle, and all they want to do right now is please me as much as I want to please her. It's as much of a rush as the gunfight earlier, but with such a greater reward.

Her hand finds my thick bulge, and I feel it send a pulse through my whole body, telling me how right she feels. I cup her face in my hand and bring our lips together. It's a gentle kiss at first, but it soon explodes into so much more. We can't keep our hands off each other. We start touching everywhere we can. Her hand strokes my cock through my pants, and I work one of my hands under her dress.

I push the fabric aside and slide two fingers into her wet pussy, feeling how desperate she is for me. She's no bystander swept up into things by chance. She's just as deadly as me in many ways, and that's such a turn-on that I've never encountered before in my life.

I start stroking her from within, dragging my

fingers up the insides of her wet depths and feeling her body shiver around my hand. Our tongues play with each other in our mouths while I finger her, and my cock pulses with desire more and more with each passing second. She's already high-strung and ready to be plucked. All it takes is for me to find the right spot.

And I do.

Color fills her cheeks as I get a steady rhythm in her, and she starts pushing her hips up in time with me. She pants through her mouth as her eyes lock onto me. I can see the windows getting steamy as I grope her breast with one hand while fingering her with the other, and I feel like this girl is totally in my power right now.

Soon, she digs her grip into the seat and my leg, and she lets her head fall back onto the seat as her whole body shudders. I can feel her come, and I stop her from squealing in delight by pressing a kiss to her lips. I feel her moan through my body as she comes, writhing in my grasp with every stroke.

Once her orgasm comes to an end, I slide my hand out of her and stick my fingers into my mouth, watching her eyes. She smiles as I lick her off me, and as soon as it's done, I open my pants to let my cock free.

It sticks straight up, swollen and ready, and Hadley knows what to do. She hikes up her dress before I can even get a grip on her, and I guide her hips toward me. She wastes no time—she knows what she wants, and what she wants is me to fill her up as soon as possible.

I pull her back down onto me, and her pussy envelops my shaft to the hilt. Even I have to let out a groan of pleasure unbidden. It's a hot, wet, over-whelming feeling that awakens every resting nerve in my body. I grip her hips and start rutting up into her without any hesitation. We're past the point of taking our time and feeling each other up. We want to fuck, and we want to do it fiercely.

My hips hammer into her hard and fast. Hadley holds onto the seat and pushes back in time with me, never losing her share of control as I pound deep into her pussy, my thick crown gliding across her g-spot over and over again. Her hair is a mess, and her gown is half draped over me, and all that disorder only makes her more enticing to me.

The cock pulsing between her legs is thicker than ever, and my balls are so swollen and sore that I've never been more eager to release inside someone. I reach up and grab her breasts from behind, fondling them and squeezing them as I rock into her. The sounds of her gasping fill the limo.

We assassinated two crime lords and are fucking in the personal limo of one of them. The rush is beyond anything I thought I'd encounter when I first came to Vegas, and now, I wouldn't trade it for anything in the world.

Hadley is teasing me as we go, clenching herself when she thinks I least expect it, trying to get me to release. My grip tightens on her, and I slide back down to her hips to remind her who's in control. But it's not that easy—Hadley and I are two people who know exactly what we want out of a lover, and we find it in each other perfectly. She's no pushover, and I'm no slacker. Our relentless, adrenaline-fueled fucking is a hot mess of all our desires wrapped up and burned so beautifully together that it's like a high.

I never want to come down from it. And with Hadley at my side, I never will.

Almost hypnotized by the rhythmic feeling of my cock sliding in and out of her with such precision, it's still no surprise when I feel Hadley starting to get tense again, ready to release. She squirms on top of me, trying desperately to keep from letting herself go. It's like a competition between us. She starts pushing her hips in such a way that I feel white-hot pleasure running through the whole length of my shaft, so close to making me release. It's a deadly tug of war that could go on forever, and I have no intention of backing down.

But our desires are our undoing. We rut into each other with such ferocity and zeal that soon, we both realize at the same time that we're about to lose control of our endurance. Hadley lets out a whimpered curse at the same time as I feel my nerves betray me, and the last warning of precum spills into her before my whole body readies itself to burst.

We come together in sweet, adrenaline-fueled bliss. My shots of hot, virile seed fill her up while her body tenses and relaxes in one unending cycle that wraps us both up and holds us together in time. I've never felt closer to another human being, and she's the only one I ever want to feel close to again.

When it's finally over, she slides slowly off my cock and flops down next to me, breathing heavily and smiling at me with lidded eyes.

"This isn't over, you know," I say to her in a thick voice. "There's still a lot of work to be done."

"If this is our idea of playing hard," she replies between breaths, "then I'll work hard with you as long as we can go."

ONE YEAR LATER

Even the smooth glass of the hotel penthouse suite window is warm against my skin as Dominick pins me against it, thrusting his cock between my legs with a forceful pulse that I can feel to my core.

I'm still pulsing from the orgasm he gave me with his tongue on the bed. I thought it couldn't get any better than that—sitting on a bed with my man's face between my legs while I look out the window at the gorgeous view of Hawaiian waters just a few yards from the hotel. The skies were endless blue, and the waters were so deep and pristine that I could get lost in them by just watching.

But Dominick has a way of making me feel loved like nothing else in the world can. His mouth is on my neck, peppering me with fierce kisses. His hands are holding me up by the hips, groping my ass while his cock impales me between my legs, so deep and fulfilling that I want to burst. Everything about him is fast and fierce.

And everything has been, since we took over the casino in Vegas.

The aftermath of the deaths of Jerry and Carl was swift and brutal. Dominick handled the political side of things. He personally took care of anyone who stood in our way and tried to bring in outside mafia leadership. We were not going to let anyone else step in and trample what we'd built, and the enforcers were sick of taking care of petty personal grudges, standing firm behind Dominick.

Once we had Jerry's casino, the rest was just a game to me. I took the other girls who were still nearby and spread out to the other casinos in the area, cleaning house and buying them out one by one.

Before we left for Hawaii, we had a total of three under our control, and more are just waiting to be plucked from the hands of the old mafia. With Dominick and I in charge and getting the respect we've fought for with our rivals, we're making waves in the city. Human trafficking has already plummeted, and I'm going to see it uprooted piece by bloody piece. Violence is down, thanks to Dominick's methods. His men are loyal, because they're being treated well, and not being asked to risk their lives for bullshit reasons.

All we have now is to sit back and rake in the staggering amounts of money flowing into our accounts, all legitimate.

It's a sweet feeling, owning what I've worked for. It's not something I ever thought I would feel, but it's so much more delicious than I ever imagined.

And I can say the same about the man thrusting between my legs right now.

My body is naked and glistening, and whenever Dominick's eyes are drinking me in, I feel more loved than I ever thought possible. I feel his thick cock sliding in and out of me, and every inch that he gives me feels like pure bliss.

I swear, he wants to fuck me on every place open to us on this island, and a lot that aren't. Since getting here, we've fucked in every place imaginable. He's taken me to a private beach and fucked me on a towel on the sand. He's had his fingers in me openly in some of the ritziest nightclubs the state has to offer. And every time we take a limo to our next destination, he either has me on his cock or his tongue between my legs.

He lifts me up until I feel his cock slide out of me, and he turns me around and presses my front to the glass. I'm exposed for the whole island to see, and the only thing keeping me from appearing on the news is the fact that we're so high up I'd be surprised if anyone could actually see me. That doesn't change the fact that I'm being pushed against glass at hundreds of feet above the ground, feeling Dominick hold my ass before he impales me again with his cock.

I let out a moan that fogs up the window as he does. My body is a mess of nerves and desire, all burning for Dominick.

I have never liked feeling controlled by anyone. Every second working for Carl was a nightmare, the more I looked back on it. Dominick knows how to dominate me in the ways I want, though, and the power games we play with each other make me feel more alive and in control than ever before.

He isn't holding anything back, but even so, I feel every inch that moves in me as if I have all the time in the world to revel in it. His crown is bulging and swollen with need to release in me, and knowing that I can instill that kind of need gives me no end of pleasure. I feel whole with him inside me, and I can love like never before.

His hands are firm and strong around me, holding me safe even as he makes me feel so very exposed and naked before the world. Each time he thrusts up into me, warmth rolls through my body. My muscles are shaking, but I don't want him to stop for anything. Even if someone walked in on us, I wouldn't stop.

And in our time, we've had some very close calls. The thought of them sends shivers up my spine.

I lose myself against the glass, closing my eyes

and thinking about every look Dominick has given me just today. The way he watches me move, the way he appreciates all the effort I put into my stride and my looks, it all makes this effort worth it. He's the only man I've ever met who can keep up with me, and being able to admit that is a rush that makes me dizzy.

Just as I feel my body getting closer to the brink of another release, I squirm, and I curse myself for it —Dominick can feel that, and he loves teasing me. He pulls me back as soon as he realizes I'm close to release, and he picks me up again.

"Damn you," I breathe with a lazy smile on my face.

He only chuckles in response, then carries me to the bed and tosses me down on it. I only have a moment to scramble to grab hold of the sheets and get on my knees before he seizes my hips, rough and bestial. The rush of Dominick coming for me when I'm so naked and vulnerable is like no other. He feels inescapable in all the best ways, and I always want him to take what he wants from me. He's fire, and I want him to consume me.

And he loves doing so.

He grabs me by the ass and drags me closer to him before he thrusts his cock deep inside me. I let out a groan of pleasure before my face hits the sheets, and I clutch the soft folds as he starts rutting into me with a fast, hard rhythm. I can hear his hips slapping against me each time, punctuated by his hot, heavy panting. He makes me feel so desired, so needed, and he expresses it with such vigor that I couldn't resist even if I wanted to.

I feel his strong hand grasp my hair and pull my head back gently, never hurting me but just firmly enough to tell me what he wants. I arch my back for him, and I can't hold back a whimper as his cock thrusts against my g-spot. He knows my body so well that he focuses on it with expert precision. One of his arms wraps around my hips to let his hand start fingering my clit while he bucks into me.

My eyes roll up and my eyelids shut as the over-whelming feelings pour in from all directions. It's almost a sensory overload, and it's everything I've ever wanted from him.

I don't realize how close I am to orgasm until he pulls me closer to him, and I feel a strong pulse roll through his cock and snap me out of my hypnotic trance into the fiery reality inside me. I whimper, biting down on the sheets and bracing myself, and this time, Dominick is ready to meet me halfway.

Just as I feel tension well up in my lower abdomen, I feel his cock thicken and stiffen one last time before we both release at the same time. His deep groan is music to my ears as I come and feel his white, thick reward empty into my depths. My heart beats fast as I push my hips back and tease every bit of it out of him that I can. I smile triumphantly as I feel his breath seize up when I clench, and he squeezes me back, rewarding me for my efforts.

It feels like it lasts forever, but I know in my heart it's probably not even the last time we're going to fuck today. It's just barely past noon.

When it's finally over, I fall to the side as he slides out of me, and we pant on the bed for a while before making eye contact again, lovingly.

"You won't be satisfied until you're just fucking me on a public beach, will you?" I tease, winking at him.

"Your words, not mine," he chuckles.

"I'm going to get cleaned up," I say, pushing myself up and swinging my legs over the edge of the bed. "The girls should be ready to meet soon. We'll have to save the lazing around in bed and staring into each other's eyes until after dinner."

"We'll see about that," he says, giving my ass a pinch from the bed. I giggle and hop away, heading to the shower with a warm blush on my cheeks.

When I step out of the shower a few minutes later with a towel wrapped around me, Dominick is already pulling a pair of jeans over his tight ass, and the way the sun makes his whole body seem to glow makes my heart warm. He turns to look at me, and the smile he shoots me is so strong I can feel it in my chest.

"Your phone lit up while you were washing off,"

he says. "Vanessa and the girls are downstairs, whenever we're ready."

"Oh god," I laugh, "I hope we didn't keep them waiting."

"No, I have a feeling they're having a good time at the bar in the meantime," he says as I hurry over to the drawer to pull on a breezy, flowy dress.

We're not in Hawaii just for a vacation on a whim. In fact, we have a couple reasons for being here, besides basking in the gorgeous sunlight and breathing in the salty, fruity breeze as long as we care to.

The first reason is the girls waiting downstairs. With Dominick's help, I've been slowly getting everyone from Carl's network together and getting them tickets to meet up here. It turns out that my hunch was right—Vanessa is not the first person Carl abused, both physically and mentally. And I'm not the only one he tried to trade to other connections in the mafia.

I tracked down girls who'd gone missing over the years, some who came and went through Carl's operation long before I even got started. Some had gone through so much abuse that when they finally got out of it, they were reluctant to come forward and dig up old trauma. But telling them that Carl was dead got some attention.

Now, I had a large group gathered here at this

hotel in Hawaii, all expenses paid by me without putting so much as a dent in my bank account.

That last part is thanks to the efforts of Dominick and me in Vegas.

We wasted no time in carrying out our plans. When Jerry went down, it started unraveling the whole network of skeezy mob casino owners throughout the city. It turned out that a lot of them were like Jerry: aging, well past their prime, and all coasting on the fear they could inspire when they were younger. They'd gone soft and lost their caution.

With me cleaning house and Dominick carrying out a hit job here and there, we soon had our own little empire forming right there in Vegas, practically overnight. Things changed fast in Vegas, and even faster when the mafia was involved. But now, we're slaves to nobody, and we work for ourselves. And with each new casino we buy out, our clout grows.

Having a dramatic, theatrical story like ours helps, too. We're not nobodies. We're the enforcer and the world-class gambler who took down Jerry acting alone, and we made the right friends at the right times. The other girls make up a big portion of those friends.

Once we're dressed, we head downstairs to the lobby, where the girls are indeed gathered at the bar together, most of them holding huge, colorful drinks and chatting with each other with smiles on their faces. Vanessa is the first to catch sight of me, and she beams broadly before waving and hurrying over to meet us at the edge of the group. Some of the other girls wave and call to us too, but nobody crowds us.

"Oh my god, I can't believe you're all actually here!" I gush, throwing my arms around Vanessa as she meets me.

"Me either," she breathes, brushing some of her hair out of her eyes. I haven't seen her this happy in a long time. "I haven't even met some of the people here. Thank you so much for getting this together."

"I've been waiting for this for a long time, trust me, it's my pleasure," I say with an equally bright grin.

"Okay, but first things first, let's see it," Vanessa says, not missing a beat.

There it is—the second reason Dominick and I are in Hawaii. I roll my eyes, but even as I do, I can't hold back the smile that immediately grows on my face whenever I get asked what Vanessa is asking me.

I hold up my hand to display the massive engagement ring Dominick put on me.

Vanessa squeals in delight and takes my hand to fawn over the ring a little while I steal a smug smile at Dominick, who is currently pretending not to be paying attention to something he's actually very proud of. I have a man who's got good taste in jewelry.

Hawaii hadn't been my first choice for a wedding —when he proposed, I thought it was appropriate that we just say 'fuck it' and get the tackiest, cheesiest Vegas wedding we could possibly find. I had a vision of something like an impersonator of an Elvis impersonator doing a drive-thru wedding from our personal armored limousine.

Dominick promised he had a better idea, and I'm glad I heard it out. We're getting married next week right here on Oahu, and I couldn't be more excited.

"I have a million questions," Vanessa says, but I hold up a hand, grinning.

"I'm sure, but so does everyone else, and I don't want to keep them waiting."

"Right, right."

"Alright, everyone," I say as I clap my hands, getting the attention of everyone in our group and stepping further into the mass of the finest card players the world has ever seen, myself included. I wait until I have everyone's attention, Dominick standing behind me like a statue, and the same daring spark in my eyes that got me involved in this lifestyle from the very beginning. "Let's take this to a conference room. I want to talk to you all about a job offer."

Killing For Her

Abducted

ABOUT THE AUTHOR

Alexis Abbott is a Wall Street Journal & USA Today bestselling author who writes about bad boys protecting their girls! Pick up her books today if you can't resist a bad boy who is a good man, and find yourself transported with super steamy sex, gritty suspense, and lots of romance.

She lives in beautiful St. John's, NL, Canada with her amazing husband.

facebook.com/abbottauthor

twitter.com/abbottauthor

instagram.com/alexisabbottauthor

bookbub.com/authors/alexis-abbott

pinterest.com/badboyromance

youtube.com/AlexisAbbott

ACKNOWLEDGMENTS

Thank you to my amazing Patrons. I'm constantly humbled and grateful for your support.

Ramona Cabrera
Melissa Hedrick
Virginia Swanson
Dawn Daughenbaugh
Don Doss
Stacie Currie

If you'd like to join them — and get my ebooks or paperbacks — you can find me here on Patreon.
https://www.patreon.com/alexisabbott

www.ingramcontent.com/pod-product-compliance
Lightning Source LLC
Chambersburg PA
CBHW021128190726
48288CB00008B/2552